WHITEOUT

WHITEOUT

W.C. MACK

Scholastic Canada Ltd.

Toronto New York London Auckland Sydney

Mexico City New Delhi Hong Kong Buenos Aires

Scholastic Canada Ltd.
604 King Street West, Toronto, Ontario M5V 1E1, Canada

Scholastic Inc.
557 Broadway, New York, NY 10012, USA

Scholastic Australia Pty Limited
PO Box 579, Gosford, NSW 2250, Australia

Scholastic New Zealand Limited
Private Bag 94407, Botany, Manukau 2163, New Zealand

Scholastic Children's Books
Euston House, 24 Eversholt Street, London NW1 1DB, UK

www.scholastic.ca

This book is a work of fiction. Names, characters, places and incidents are either the product of the author's imagination or are used fictitiously, and any resemblance to actual persons, living or dead, business establishments, events or locales is entirely coincidental.

Library and Archives Canada Cataloguing in Publication
Mack, W. C., 1972-, author
    Whiteout / W.C. Mack.
Issued in print and electronic formats.
ISBN 978-1-4431-4868-9 (softcover).--
ISBN 978-1-4431-4869-6 (ebook)
    I. Title.
PS8625.A24W45 2018   jC813'.6   C2017-904992-5
                                          C2017-904993-3

If you purchased this book without a cover, you should be aware that this book is stolen property. It was reported as "unsold and destroyed" to the publisher, and neither the author nor the publisher has received any payment for this "stripped book."

Cover photo © yulkapopkova/iStockphoto

6 5 4 3 2 1   Printed in Canada   139   18 19 20 21 22

For my best friend, Mike Smith, who came up with the title, the concept, and pushed me to write this book. Thank you!

CHAPTER ONE

I pulled the carefully rolled posters out of their cardboard tube, hoping they'd survived the trip from Kansas.

They were still in mint condition. No rips, no folds, no creases.

Whew!

I took off the rubber bands that held them together and flattened the stack out on the floor of my new bedroom.

I had thick blue carpet this time, and blinds instead of frilly curtains, which was cool. I even had a walk-in closet for all my gear. I knew from experience that things could have been a lot worse.

I knelt down on the floor to flip through my poster collection. Other than my family, it was the only thing in my life that never changed.

On top of the pile was a shot of Christian Vigo in the middle of his Backside 720 from the Snowboarding Grand Prix in Mammoth. Next up was Matty Doakes in the coolest Oakley jacket ever, holding a bronze Olympic medal and smiling like he'd conquered the world (which he almost had!) Underneath that was one of my favourites: D-Day with nothing but bright blue sky around him as he pulled a Fastplant Frontflip at the Winter X Games.

Now *that* was sick.

Wait. Did they say sick in Oregon?

Or did they say awesome, sweet, cool or something else? Something I'd never even heard before?

I'd find out soon enough. School started at eight o'clock the next morning, and my stomach was already knotted up. I wasn't ready for another new school. I'd barely gotten used to the last one.

I turned to the next poster and stared at Cody White's face, grinning back at me like he didn't have a single thing to worry about.

Why couldn't *I* be a pro snowboarder?

I wouldn't have to make friends because I'd already have teammates. And I'd be famous, so regular people would automatically want to hang out with me. And school? I could have a tutor or something, like movie stars do, and I'd never have to be the new kid in a classroom again. *Ever.*

I weighed down the poster corners with a pencil

case, two unmatched sneakers and the Cody White book I'd read over and over again.

As much as I loved the book, I couldn't help hoping I'd have a little less time to read in Oregon.

I wanted to be busy with friends.

Which meant I had to *make* friends.

I knew from seven moves in five years that the only way that might happen was if I looked and sounded like everybody else.

But I had no idea what everybody else looked or sounded *like* at Evergreen Middle School.

Catching up with Math, English or any of my other subjects was a total breeze, but preparing for life in the hallway and cafeteria? That was something else.

If there was a way to study for a new social life, I would have happily crammed all night.

At least it wouldn't be too tough to learn my way around town. Timber only had two gas stations, a bank, a library, a grocery store, a Mexican restaurant and a Dairy Queen. That was a lot less than most of the places I'd lived, which was kind of nice.

Then again, there was only one middle school, which meant there were fewer kids to try making friends with too.

"Whatcha doing?" Thomas asked, from my open doorway.

My little brother didn't have the same problem I did. No matter where Dad's job took us, the kid always had a handful of friends on the first day. By lunch. People liked him right away, and the most annoying part was he didn't even have to try.

"Getting my room ready," I told him.

"You're gonna put all the same stuff up *again*?"

"Yup." In exactly the same places. Just like last time and the time before that and the time before that. Those posters made me feel at home, even if the place was only mine for a little while.

"My room's pink," Thomas muttered.

"More like light brown," I said.

He raised one eyebrow. "It has a Minnie Mouse light switch."

He had me there. "Okay, it's pink," I admitted. "But maybe the landlord will let us paint it."

"Maybe," he said.

"Two bathrooms. Better than the last place."

"Better? I don't have enough outlets and I can't find a power bar for my Xbox."

"Set it up downstairs," I suggested.

He shook his head. "Mom probably won't let me. She hates *Zombieville*." He scratched his head. "And *Alien Blasters*. And *Vampire Assassin*. Have you seen my headset?"

"Nope," I told him, glad that he couldn't find it. My brother spent more time playing video games with total strangers all over the country than he spent talking to his own family.

He looked at me for a couple of seconds, then asked, "So, are you ready for tomorrow?"

"I guess so," I told him, with a shrug.

Was I ready for thirty sets of eyes staring at me when I was introduced in homeroom? Was I ready to spend most of the day lost and late for classes? To hear a hundred whispers call me "new kid"? Just like Libertyville and Benton, they'd *probably* still call me new kid if I lived there until I was a hundred. I'd never be *from* there.

I sighed. I'd never be from anywhere.

"You don't have to walk me to school, you know," Thomas said. "It's cool."

I glanced up at him. Like every waking minute of his life, he was a total mess. His hair was sticking up all over the place, he had either dirt or chocolate (or both) smeared on his face and I counted three pink toes sticking out of the holes in his socks. His "So What?" T-shirt was a perfect fit.

"Yeah, I do," I told him. "Mom said."

Thomas rolled his eyes. "I'm not a baby, Steven. I can walk a couple of blocks by myself."

This might sound crazy, but I *wanted* to walk my eleven-year-old brother to the elementary school. Those few minutes would probably be the only time all day that I talked to anyone who wasn't a teacher.

It stunk that *I* was supposed to be the leader of the two of us. *I* was supposed to be the cool one who didn't want to hang out with my little brother. And yet, Thomas had always seemed older than me. It wasn't that he was smarter (although sometimes he was), but that he'd always been more confident. He was comfortable with how he looked and who he was. He didn't care what people thought.

Unless . . .

Was he worried that I'd embarrass him?

"*Thomas*," Mom said from the hallway. "You're walking with Steven."

I didn't know why we were even *going* to school at all. One stinking week, right before Christmas break? There was no point.

"I'm eleven, Mom," he reminded her.

She appeared in the doorway. "I'm aware of that. In case you've forgotten, I was going to drop you both off and you were horrified at the thought."

"Because it would be totally humiliating," I reminded her.

"Yeah," Thomas agreed. "No one else's *mommy* is going to be there."

"And we all agreed on a compromise," she said, firmly. "That you two would walk to school together."

"Why can't we just stay here?" I asked.

"I'm going to be running all kinds of errands. As we've already discussed, you don't want to come and I'm not leaving you here in an empty house, in an unfamiliar town."

"We'll stay inside," Thomas promised.

"Playing video games," she countered.

"What's wrong with video games?" he asked.

"I wouldn't be sitting in here," I told her. "I'd be snowboarding."

"Not by yourself," Mom argued.

"Seriously? I'm *thirteen*, Mom. Way too old for the buddy system."

"There's no age limit for the buddy system, Steven. It's a matter of safety and common sense."

"Okay, okay. But Mom, the runs are going to be *so* clear this week. Once Christmas break starts, the whole world is going to be swarming the mountain."

Mom sighed. "The topic is closed."

"But Mom—"

"You are *not* missing a week of school. Period."

"Fine," I sighed, giving up.

"And Steven?" she said, heading back into the hallway. "Let's get some clothes laid out for the morning, okay?"

"I will. I just want to get these posters up first."

She poked her head into the room again. "Decorating can wait."

"It's not decorating, it's—"

"Not a priority right now," she interrupted. "We're not scrambling around looking for clean jeans in the morning."

"I know," I told her. "I'll be ready."

7

When I was alone again, I moved the posters to my bare mattress and started unpacking my clothes. It was best to blend in on the first day, so I dug out a pair of jeans that were almost clean and my favourite Burton hoodie. There was snow on the ground, but I wouldn't be caught dead in rubber boots, so I found the missing shoe from my pair of Vans and set them next to my bed.

My hair had grown out from a buzz and it was at that weird in-between stage, so I went through my beanies and picked a plain black one. I looked everything over and nodded. It was safe.

"Steven, Thomas!" Mom called about twenty minutes later, just as I was tacking Eli Taylor up next to the window. "Dinner!"

When I made it downstairs, I was amazed that she'd managed to pull the whole kitchen together in the same amount of time it took me to hang a few posters.

"Spaghetti?" Thomas asked, handing his empty plate to Mom. "Awesome."

"I'm glad you approve," she said, smiling.

When it was my turn, Mom loaded up my plate with noodles, sauce and three fat meatballs.

"Thanks, Mom," I said, grabbing the seat next to my brother.

Just as I started to twirl noodles onto my fork, the front door opened.

"Dad!" Thomas shouted, through his mouthful.

"How are we doing?" Dad asked, stomping the snow off his boots as a gust of cold air made goosebumps pop up on my arms. "Smells fantastic in here."

"Spaghetti," I explained, reaching for a piece of Mom's garlic bread, which was the best I'd ever tasted.

Dad closed the door and took off his coat, then grabbed an empty plate to carry over to the pot.

"I can get it," he said, when Mom reached for the scoop. Thomas and I pretended not to notice when he kissed her.

"Did you get them?" I asked Dad as soon as he and Mom joined us at the table.

"They're in my coat pocket," he said, nodding. "Season passes for all of us."

"Awesome," I said, grinning. Free passes were the best thing about Dad working for the mountain.

Unlimited access meant I'd be spending every minute I wasn't stuck in the classroom on my board. And every minute out there practising brought me one step closer to being a pro.

What if I had posters of *myself* to hang on my walls one day?

Okay, that would be kind of weird . . . but kind of awesome, too.

"How was the office?" Mom asked.

"Good." Dad pierced a meatball with his fork. "Vikki showed me around and everyone seems nice."

Sometimes I forgot that Dad was a "new guy" too.

He worked for the Forest Service and he got moved around a lot, depending on where they needed people. Every time he transferred, he had a new group of co-workers, a new office and new duties. And Mom would be looking for a brand new job as soon as we'd all settled in.

I looked up at the dark wood ceilings, liking the cabin feel of the house. It was a lot cooler than the apartment we had back in Kansas.

"By the way," Dad said, interrupting my thoughts. "I saw something at the office that might interest you."

"What?"

He wiggled his eyebrows. "An autographed picture of Cody White, taken right here on the mountain."

"No way," I gasped.

"Way," he answered, with a laugh.

"Pulling a Double Mondo?"

"Now that, I don't know."

"It's his trademark."

"A double what?" Mom asked.

"Mondo. You saw one on my *Whiteout* DVD."

"The one you've watched a hundred times?" Thomas asked, rolling his eyes.

"More like a thousand, but yeah." And I'd watch it again, as soon as the computer was set up. Once Thomas got his Xbox unpacked, he would totally dominate the TV. "Do you think he'll come back?" I asked Dad.

"Your guess is as good as mine, Steven," he said, spinning noodles onto his fork.

"I hope so." I grinned. "Can you imagine a pro, right in our backyard?"

I didn't wait for an answer from anyone at the table. I was too busy daydreaming about hauling down the same runs as Cody White or any of the pros in my pile of posters.

What if the only thing I had to think about every morning was which board I'd use or which goggles I'd wear?

I smiled as I spun some more noodles onto my fork, saving the juicy and delicious meatballs for last.

For the rest of the night, all I could think about was the fact that Cody White had stood just a quarter of a mile away from where I was sitting.

That is, until I got ready for bed. I had only a few hours left before school started, and my nerves were working overtime.

I changed into my pyjamas and looked at my walls, half-covered with legends.

I bet D-Day never had to worry about starting at a new school. Or Toby Briggs. I sighed, lifting the rest of the posters onto my bed so I could look through them. And there he was: Cody White, with his super-blond, curly hair streaming out of the back of his helmet.

"That design is pretty cool," Thomas said, from my doorway. He was pointing at the jagged "White" splatter on the bottom of the board. "You should ask for that one for Christmas. I mean, you're a White too."

"Yeah." My Christmas list was already pretty long and knowing how much some of the gear cost, adding a new board would be pointless.

And if I was going to add one, it would be the Burton I'd seen in their catalogue. It was bright green, with graffiti-style drawings all over it. I'd never seen one like it and I'd fallen in love on the spot.

It was called the Green Beast.

"Wouldn't it be cool if we were related to him?" Thomas asked.

"Huh?" Was he still talking about Cody White?

"Steven?" Thomas asked. "Wouldn't it be cool?"

"Yeah, but . . ." I started to say, then the most amazing idea popped into my head. "That's it!" I gasped.

"What?"

My mind had gone from zero to sixty in about two seconds.

It was *perfect!*

"What?" he asked again.

"Never mind." All of the pieces were clicking into place and I didn't have time to explain.

"Whatever." He shrugged.

I glanced up at the Cody White poster and knew that I was on to something.

Something awesome.

I wasn't going to be the anonymous kid who got bumped into lockers and didn't know his way to homeroom. I wasn't going to be the guy no one wanted to take a chance on in gym class or sit next to in the cafeteria.

I wasn't going to be known only as "new kid" until we moved away again.

I had a master plan, and for the first time I could remember, I was actually looking forward to my first day of school.

And it was all because of a blinding flash of pure genius.

I was going to be instantly cool.

I was going to be unbelievably popular.

I was going to be Cody White's cousin.

CHAPTER TWO

When the alarm went off in the morning, I rolled over to hit the off button but my palm slid onto something slippery instead.

I opened one eye and squinted in the darkness.

My stack of *Transworld Snowboarder* magazines.

What were they doing there?

I opened the other eye, totally confused until it hit me.

Oh yeah. We're in Oregon now.

I found the alarm clock and turned it off, feeling that same old sick sense of dread in my stomach.

New town, new school. New everything.

I stared at the ceiling, feeling miserable for just a couple of seconds before I remembered my master plan.

I smiled in the darkness as the dread disappeared.

This time was going to be different.

This time, I was in control.

Excited, I jumped out of bed and into the shower, humming all the way. When I got dressed in my under-the-radar clothes and looked in the mirror, I decided I'd made pretty solid choices.

I looked cool and maybe even a little mysterious.

I pulled on my beanie and headed downstairs.

"Now that's a smile I didn't expect to see this morning," Dad said, lifting his coffee mug at me like he was making a toast. "What's going on?"

"Nothing," I said, with a shrug.

"No first-day jitters?" he asked, obviously surprised.

"Nope," I said, dropping two pieces of bread into the toaster.

"Well, that's good news," he said, patting me on the back as he hit up the coffee pot for a refill.

By the time my toast popped, Thomas was digging in the bread bag, looking for the dry ends of the loaf.

"So, Big T," Dad said, "are you ready to take on the world?"

"Sure," my brother answered, tearing a slice in half and shoving it into his mouth.

"Want some peanut butter with that?" I asked.

"Nope," he said, in between chews.

I poured myself some orange juice and spread thick layers of peanut butter, then jelly, on my toast.

As I bit into the crunchy, creamy goodness, I thought about how impressed the kids at school would be when they heard I was a celebrity. Well, related to one, anyway.

Why hadn't I come up with the Cody White plan sooner? It would have saved me all kinds of grief.

"You boys ready?" Mom asked, squeezing my shoulder as she made her way to the coffee pot.

"Yup," Thomas and I said at the same time.

A moment later, I watched her take a slow sip of coffee with her eyes closed. I was glad there wasn't anything I needed *that* badly in the morning. (Other than snow and my board, anyway.)

"I'm serious about you two walking together," she reminded us. "And I mean joined at the hip."

I nodded and Thomas rolled his eyes.

When we were finished with breakfast, we kissed Mom goodbye, grabbed our backpacks and waved to Dad as we headed out the door.

"Fresh snow," Thomas said, as he led the way down the driveway.

"Nice!" What was better than having a season pass *and* living practically on the mountain?

Absolutely nothing.

I followed my little brother down to Pine Street, daydreaming about strapping on my board and hitting the lift as soon as the final bell rang.

"You nervous?" Thomas asked, once the elementary school was in sight.

"Nope."

His head whipped around. "Really?"

I nodded, shoving my hands deeper into my pockets. I should have worn gloves. They might not look cool, but they'd save my fingers. "Really."

He gave me a long look, probably remembering all of the first days that came before this one. All the times I probably looked like I was going to puke (and did, twice).

"How come?"

"What?"

He shrugged. "How come you aren't nervous this time?"

For some reason, I didn't want to tell him about my plan, my White Lie, as I was beginning to think of it.

"I don't know," I told him. "I guess I've been through it so many times, it doesn't bug me anymore."

He gave me another long look, but didn't push it.

When we reached the Cedar Elementary gate, we skipped the hugs and just nodded at each other instead. Then we went our separate ways.

I couldn't help turning to watch him head down the walkway. Before he was even halfway to the front door, he'd joined a group of kids and was already laughing like he'd known them forever.

I smiled, knowing I would follow in his footsteps in just a couple of blocks.

"Right!" someone shouted from behind me, but before I could turn around I was almost knocked to the ground by a kid on a bicycle.

"Hey!" I shouted after him, then muttered, "Jerk."

The brakes squealed and he kicked up a rooster tail of snow as he stopped and turned around to face me.

Within seconds, another bike whipped past me and pulled up beside him.

Both riders turned to face me, scowling.

Uh-oh.

"What's your deal?" the first one asked. "I said *right*."

I nodded.

"That means you're supposed to go *left* to get out of the way," he sneered.

"Idiot," the other kid said, shaking his head.

Before I could say anything, they took off toward the school, laughing all the way.

I was the idiot? Who rode bikes in the *snow*? I watched one of them skid and slide on an icy patch and hoped he would wipe out. But of course he didn't.

I kicked the snow, ticked off at myself for acting the way I always did. Sure, keeping quiet had been the safe thing to do in the past, but was safe enough? Keeping my mouth shut had kept me out of fights and junk like that, but had it actually done anything *for* me? Had it made me any friends?

No.

I kept walking, determined to turn things around.

Who did those guys think they were, anyway?

I wasn't an idiot. I was Cody White's cousin.

"Cody White's cousin," I whispered to myself, smiling.

As I walked down the path, pairs and groups of kids came from all sides, heading in the same direction. A lot of the girls looked the same as the ones in Kansas. Same backpacks, same ponytails, same giggling. I tried to catch up to a group of guys, but when I got within earshot, it wasn't tricks or runs they were talking about, but TV shows, homework and basketball.

A town at the base of a mountain had to be the home to some snowboarders, didn't it? There had to be *someone* I could start a conversation with about the best runs, Cody White's last visit or the upcoming Winter X Games.

I saw a kid with a long striped scarf wrapped around his neck about a thousand times walking by himself, and matched his pace.

"Hi," he said, glancing at me with curiosity.

"Hi," I replied, with a big smile.

"Are you new?"

"Yeah. I'm Steven."

"I'm Ethan."

"Cool," I said, glad to at least be talking to someone. "You snowboard?"

He shook his head. "No, but my family snowshoes on the weekends."

"What about skiing?"

"Nah."

"Any other sports? Like, school teams?"

"Nope. I'm in the Evergreen music program, though."

It wasn't exactly what I'd hoped to talk about, but it was better than nothing. "Really?"

That was all the encouragement he needed to start talking about the Christmas concert scheduled for Friday, the spring musical and a bunch of other stuff.

I tried to concentrate on what he was saying, but I was really just waiting for the opportunity to mention my famous "cousin." The sooner I got that news out there, the better.

But I couldn't get a word in, especially when Ethan got started on his role as the Scarecrow in *The Wizard of Oz* last year.

I'd definitely picked the wrong kid.

While he yakked, I scanned the crowd, looking for anyone who might be a bit more like me. I didn't see any obvious snowboarding gear, which made it tough.

The closer we got to the front doors of the school, the more aware I was that the clock was ticking. The downside of moving to town right before a holiday was that I'd only have until Friday to make friends. Otherwise, I'd be spending the whole two-week break on my own.

"See ya," Ethan said, entering the school.

It was now or never.

I took a deep breath on my way through the front

door, hoping things were about to turn around.

But when I walked in, it smelled exactly the same as every other school, like a mixture of old lunch meat, sneakers and bleach.

"Watch out," a boy said, as he bumped into me.

I stepped out of the way and collided with a girl who gave me a dirty look when I said I was sorry.

The chatter bounced off the walls and I could barely hear myself think in the hallway. I stopped in front of a bulletin board covered with signs about upcoming basketball games, the Christmas concert Ethan had mentioned and a fundraiser for the library.

It turned out that the school mascot was a lumberjack called Larry.

Larry the Lumberjack.

Really.

I stuck close to the wall as bodies pushed past me, and I unfolded the schedule the principal gave me when Mom and I visited the main office for registration. I had a basic idea of how everything worked, so it was just a matter of jumping in. Taking a deep breath, I started walking again, searching for the numbers of my homeroom class.

I'd deal with finding my locker later.

When I arrived at Mrs. Hawthorne's room, I grabbed the first empty desk, hoping it wasn't assigned seating. I dropped my pack on the floor and leaned back to check out my surroundings. Judging by the number of maps on the walls, either Mrs. Hawthorne really liked to travel, or she taught Social Studies.

"Are you new?" a girl's voice asked from behind me.

I spun around in my seat. "Yup."

The girl, who had curly brown hair and wore a pink sweatshirt with way too much glitter on it, smiled. "Cool. We don't get a lot of new kids. Where are you from?"

Glitter or not, at least she was friendly.

"All over the place," I told her, then started listing off states. Her eyes widened as I finally ended with my most recent home. Kansas.

"Great," a boy groaned from my other side. "A new kid."

I turned to face him and recognized the guy who'd almost run me over on his bike. "Hi, I'm—"

"Boring," he said, with a yawn I was pretty sure was fake.

I could tell right away that he was just like Jackson in Libertyville, who used to start food fights in the cafeteria. Or Benjamin Withers, the bully back in Springfield, who used to shove the smaller kids into lockers.

Did every school in every town have one of these guys, just waiting to pick on somebody else?

"Don't be a creep, Nolan," the girl said.

Surprised, I was smiling at her when the bike rider's buddy appeared next to him.

Great. Evergreen had two of them.

"You again?" he asked.

"Yeah, I'm Steven," I told them, but they weren't listening.

"He's from Kansas," Nolan said, with a smirk.

What was wrong with Kansas?

"You ski?" the other guy asked.

"The dude is from *Kansas*, Tyler," Nolan said, with a laugh.

"I'm from a lot of places," I told them, trying not to get flustered. "And I'm a boarder."

Nolan snorted. "Snowboarding's for losers."

I couldn't believe what I was hearing! "Uh, try telling that to D-Day, Matty Doakes or Cody White."

I glanced out the window, wishing I was up on that snow-covered mountain. If I was a pro, I'd never have to deal with jerks like this!

"Like I care about Cody White," Nolan sneered.

What? He couldn't be serious.

"Are you kidding me? The guy's won medals for snowboarding *and* skateboarding and—"

"Who are you, his mom?" Nolan sneered.

"No, I'm . . ." I took a deep breath, amazed that he'd given me the perfect opening so soon. It was now or never. "I'm his cousin."

I waited for gasps of shock and awe, but there was silence.

"Yeah, right," Tyler said, rolling his eyes.

"You're a liar," Nolan agreed.

"No, I'm—"

Before I could say anything more, a woman with short dark hair and bright green glasses walked into the room and everyone stopped talking.

"Steven?" she asked, scanning the room. "Steven White?"

"See?" I heard the glitter girl whisper to the jerks. "Steven *White*."

I raised my hand so Mrs. Hawthorne could see me.

"Ah, there you are. I just wanted to make sure you found your way this morning."

"I did," I said, as what felt like about a thousand pairs of eyes turned to stare at me.

When she looked down at her papers, Nolan covered his mouth with his hand and coughed, "Liar."

A few people giggled and I felt my cheeks burn with embarrassment.

What was I thinking? No one was going to believe I was related to a superstar just because I *said so*.

But how could I prove it?

"Mr. White?" Mrs. Hawthorne said.

"Yes?"

"This school has a no-hat policy."

"Oh."

A couple of kids snickered and my face got even hotter.

For a split second, I worried about being stuck with

hat-head for the rest of the day. But then I realized taking off the beanie was perfect.

As all of the kids stared, I yanked it off my head, exposing my half-grown-out buzz cut.

Now, people freaked, seeing what had been hidden underneath.

I'd never been so happy to have super-blond hair!

It was even lighter than Cody's, and even though my *curls* weren't quite as crazy as his, it was close enough.

They believed me.

My plan was a total success, and by lunchtime, I actually had kids asking me to sit at their table. No, more like *begging* me to sit at their table.

I was loving every second of it.

As I walked through the cafeteria, all I heard was whispering around me. And it wasn't the kind of whispering I was used to. It was more like . . . amazement.

"What's he like?" some kid asked me as soon as I sat down at an empty space on a bench. I took a huge bite of a steaming burrito, which burned the roof of my mouth, but I chewed nice and slowly anyway, savouring the moment.

"Cody?" I asked, once I'd swallowed.

"Duh," he said, laughing.

I smiled. I knew more about Cody White and the rest of the pros than anyone. I'd watched every televised competition I could, I owned practically every snowboarding DVD ever made, recorded every interview and I'd read my tattered copy of White's biography at least a hundred times. It was like I'd spent my whole life studying for this moment.

"He's awesome," I said, taking another bite of my scorching hot burrito. I took my time chewing and swallowing again, wishing lunch would last forever.

"Does he wear his own clothes?" another kid asked.

"You mean from his clothing line? Sure, but he mostly wears stuff from his sponsors," I told him, thinking of all the magazine photos I'd seen. "You know, Volcom, Oakley."

"Birdhouse," a short kid with braces said, nodding.

Whew! At least one kid at Evergreen knew that Cody White was a skateboarder too. That was something.

"Yeah." I took another bite of my burrito, glad it was starting to cool off.

But the questions were just heating up.

"What kind of music does he like?"

"How often does he practise?"

"Who does he hang out with?"

Thanks to my obsession, I was able to answer every single question they fired at me. I even knew how many flavours of Cody White gum existed (not that anyone asked).

The crowd of kids kept growing and I couldn't stop smiling.

If they wanted to talk to Steven White, they had to get in line!

For the first time ever, I was popular.

It was awesome.

That is, until somebody asked, "When was the last time you saw him?"

I hadn't expected *that*. I took my time chewing and swallowing. "Last Christmas," I finally said, figuring it was believable enough. "We, uh, all got together for the holidays." I saw the looks on their faces and couldn't help adding, "like usual."

I swear the gasps sucked all of the air out of the cafeteria.

"Like usual?" a girl with thick glasses asked.

"Yeah," I said, then realized my mistake.

I'd totally forgotten that Christmas was less than two weeks away!

"Is he coming *here*?" several voices asked at once.

"Uh, no."

A few people groaned.

"What did he give you last year?" a girl with a long ponytail asked.

I swallowed hard. "You mean for Christmas?" My mind was racing. "We don't exchange gifts."

"Hold on," the kid with the braces said. "Your millionaire cousin doesn't give you Christmas presents?"

"He's more like a billionaire," the girl with the ponytail said.

"Or a gazillionaire," someone chimed in from the back of the crowd.

"He's lying," a voice I recognized as Nolan's said loudly. "About all of it."

That was all it took for some of the kids . . . my *fans* . . . to start drifting away from the table. I could practically feel my popularity balloon deflating with a sickening wheeze.

"No!" I shouted, panicked. I took a deep breath. "I'm not lying. He's my cousin. We're cousins." I scrambled for something, *anything,* that would make them stay. "He let me have one of his Powder Fest medals," I blurted. "One of the golds."

Everyone went quiet and still as they stared at me.

"Not to keep forever or anything," I quickly added. "I'm just holding on to it for a while."

It worked! The crowd gathered close again and I was sure I'd made the perfect move.

That is, until Nolan said, "So, bring it in tomorrow."

"What?" I practically choked.

"Bring it in tomorrow to show us," he said, with an evil smile.

What was I supposed to do?

"Bring it in?" I repeated, quietly.

"It's *proof*," Nolan said. "And we need proof."

CHAPTER THREE

I barely listened to a word my teachers said during my afternoon classes. I was too busy kicking myself for messing up my popularity already. Being cool had lasted for a couple of hours, tops, and pretty soon I would be branded not only a loser, but a *liar*.

It wasn't fair!

Or was it? The jury wasn't in on the loser part, but I had to admit that I *was* technically a liar.

How was I going to save myself from total humiliation the next morning?

A Powder Fest gold medal?

Why couldn't I have said I had an autographed picture of Cody? At least that was something I could borrow from Dad's office. Why did I have to pick something that would be one hundred percent *impossible* to replicate?

When the final bell rang, I loaded my pack at my locker and listened to the kids around me talking about basketball practice.

Basketball?

The town was at the base of one of the best snowboarding mountains around and they were talking about *basketball*?

It was insane.

I pulled my hat back on and started toward the door.

"See you tomorrow," a couple of kids said, while others waved or nodded at me.

It was the most attention I'd ever gotten on a first day of school, which counted for something. Then again, it was only because of my stupid lie, which counted for even more.

Why did my master plan have to be such a total failure?

As I headed for Cedar Elementary to meet Thomas and walk home together, I tried to think of a way to salvage my popularity.

It wasn't like I could pick up a Powder Fest medal at the local sporting goods shop. And if by some miracle there was one for sale on eBay, I wouldn't be able to afford it and couldn't get it by the next day anyway.

I shook my head, wishing I'd never opened my big mouth.

"Steven!" I heard Thomas shout when I reached his school.

I waved at him and waited.

When he reached me, he was out of breath but smiling.

"I can't go snowboarding with you," he gasped.

We'd made plans the night before to hit the mountain as soon as school got out! "What do you mean, you *can't*?"

"I mean I don't want to," he said, shrugging. "I'm going to a friend's house to play *Space Chase*."

"A video game?" I asked.

He'd rather play *video games* than race with me down brand new runs? The kid had to be an alien or something.

"Not just a video game, Steven. It's *Space Chase*. Ben got it yesterday."

"Who's Ben?"

Wait a second. He was already invited to a friend's house? It was like Kansas all over again.

Except this time, it was messing up my snowboarding plans.

"That guy." He pointed to a kid at the edge of the parking lot. "He's in my class."

There was no way Mom would let him go to a stranger's house on the first day of school. And that was a good thing, because we had to use the buddy system for snowboarding. Yes, it was totally insane, but if Thomas didn't go, I couldn't go.

I shook my head. "Mom's not going to let you—"

"She already said it was okay."

"What? How?"

"I forgot my lunch and I asked her when she dropped it off."

"But you can't—"

"Yeah, I can," he said, walking backwards toward Ben. "I'll see you at dinner," he called over his shoulder as he turned away.

I couldn't believe it! I'd been dying to get out on my board. I needed to ride, so I could clear my head.

I started walking toward home, totally ticked off and disappointed. I was so distracted, I didn't hear the footsteps behind me until a guy fell into step next to me.

"Hey," he said.

It was the one who'd known about Birdhouse in the cafeteria.

"Hey," I replied, and nodded casually, like kids approached me every day.

"Where do you live?"

"Pine."

"Street, Avenue or Loop?" he asked, laughing. "We've got Pine everything." He shoved his hands into his pockets. They were bare like mine and probably just as frozen.

"Street," I told him.

"Cool. You're going my way."

For the first time ever, I had someone other than

my little brother to walk home with on the first day of school.

That was almost enough to make me forget about the huge mess I'd created.

Almost.

"What's your name?" I asked, as we turned onto Commercial Street.

"Carlos."

"I'm Steven," I told him.

"I know. Steven *White*," he said, grinning. "You're already kind of famous around here."

"Yeah," I said, realizing that after I failed to bring in the gold medal, he probably wouldn't want to walk with me again. I'd have to enjoy it while it lasted.

"Where'd you move here from?"

"Kansas," I told him, then listed off the states that came before it.

"Man, that would be so cool," he said.

"What?"

"Living in other places."

"Never for very long, though," I told him.

"Even better," he said. "You could start over and be whoever you want."

I shook my head. "It's not that easy. I wish I'd lived in one place my whole life."

"No you don't," Carlos said, laughing. "I've been in Timber since I was born. It's the same thing, every day. The only thing that's changed is the Dairy Queen." He

33

glanced at me, then explained, "It used to be a Wendy's."

We were quiet for a little bit, until Carlos asked, "You snowboard?"

"Yeah, you?"

"I'm more of a skater," he said.

"Oh." I tried to hide my disappointment, but it was tough.

"We've got a half-pipe in a little skate park outside of town that'll open up in the spring."

"Nice," I said. Then I couldn't help asking, "So, you don't board at all?"

"Every now and then," he said. "It's too expensive."

I knew exactly what he meant. Between the gear and the lift ticket, the costs really added up. That's why I was so glad Dad worked for the mountain.

"You don't have a pass?" I asked.

"Nope."

I would have offered to let him use Thomas's so he could go with me sometime, but our passes had our photos on them.

As we walked, snow started falling, and with every flake that floated past me, I felt a bit better about everything. I was already halfway to making a new friend, which was epic (even if the friendship was doomed to end after one day).

I was about to ask if he wanted to come over and hang out when Carlos asked, "So, you think you could get me an autograph?"

I swallowed hard, knowing exactly what he meant. "Cody White's autograph?"

He laughed. "Yeah."

I didn't even have one of those. I'd written letters to a couple of his sponsors, asking for one, but never heard anything back. If I couldn't get one for myself, how was I supposed to get one for Carlos?

"Cody White's autograph," I repeated, more quietly.

"Why do you always say his whole name?" he asked.

"What?"

Carlos shrugged. "He's your cousin. Why don't you just call him Cody?"

Was there *any* part of this master plan that I'd thought all the way through? I was messing the whole thing up so fast, it was unbelievable.

"I'll see what I can do," I told him. "About the autograph, I mean."

"Sweet," Carlos said, grinning.

I thought again about inviting him to my house, but he'd probably want to see pictures of Cody and me together. Or worse, he'd want to see the gold medal I didn't have.

What was I thinking when I told that stupid lie?

The answer was obvious. I wasn't thinking at all.

Carlos and I talked about our favourite videos on our way home, and when we reached Pine Street, he kind of stood there, like he was waiting for me to invite him over.

"I'll see you later," I said.

"Yeah, tomorrow morning. I'll catch you here around eight," he said. "We can walk in together."

"Cool." I nodded, trying not to look too excited.

As I walked up the driveway, I thought about the fact that I'd had the best first day of school *ever* and tried to forget that my second would probably be my worst.

How was I going to get out of the medal mess?

Mom wasn't home, so I dug my front door key out of my pocket and let myself in.

I dumped my pack by the laundry room and headed straight for the fridge, wondering if there was any left-over spaghetti. But when I walked into the kitchen, I stopped in my tracks when I saw the snow-covered peak through the window.

It was practically begging me to grab my gear.

"Stupid buddy system," I groaned, wishing Mom and Dad would let me do stuff on my own.

I opened the fridge and found the contents pretty disappointing. Unless I wanted to make a tuna sandwich or scramble some eggs, I was out of luck.

I peeked out the window again and sighed.

What was I supposed to do at three in the afternoon?

Homework? I didn't have any yet.

Clean my room? Most of my stuff was still in boxes.

Oh, I guess I could unpack.

Nah.

Was there anything I could use to make a gold medal?

I shook my head, sure I was nuts for even entertaining the possibility. Mom and Dad didn't have gold bars stashed in the garage. I was pretty sure we didn't even have gold *paint*. And who was I kidding? A guy who could barely handle a class art project in sixth grade couldn't make a Powder Fest medal to save his life (well, his social life, anyway).

There was some microwave popcorn in the pantry, so I nuked a bag and ate it in front of the TV. I clicked through the channels, but nothing good was on and I ended up staring out the window at that mountain.

The snow was an almost-blinding white in the afternoon sun.

I rinsed my bowl and put it in the dishwasher, wishing Thomas had just come home with me.

Why did we even use the stupid buddy system? My little brother was only eleven, so what could he do if we ran into trouble? And what kind of trouble did my parents really expect us to get into out in the middle of a run, anyway?

"Forget this," I muttered, turning off the TV and heading upstairs. I had at least an hour and a half before my parents would be home, and I sure wasn't going to spend it watching some dumb TV show and dreading my second day at Evergreen.

I ran upstairs, happy to see my lift pass hanging on my bedroom doorknob. It only took me a couple of minutes to grab my gear from the huge closet and get out the door.

I was going for it.

The walk over to the lift only took a few minutes, and the line was short, which was awesome. I watched two girls get on the chair. They were giggling about something and I wished I had someone to laugh with too. I wished my brother wasn't the biggest social butterfly in the Western Hemisphere.

While I waited my turn, I watched the action at the base. There was a kiddie ski class in session and I smiled when I heard the instructor telling them to turn their skis into a piece of pie. That was exactly how Dad had taught me when I was about four.

I could still remember skiing in between his legs, my tiny pie piece surrounded by his big one.

Dad had been kind of sad when I made the switch to snowboarding, but I couldn't help the fact that I totally loved it. Once I got on a board for the first time, there was no turning back (unless it was to pull a Shifty Rewind or something).

I watched a couple of people wipe out as they came to the end of a green run. I winced, even though they were obviously beginners and had probably fallen a hundred times in the last hour.

I turned toward the map of all the runs and saw

some double black diamonds. The ultimate.

Was I ready for a double black diamond run?

Absolutely.

I could already picture myself catching air and cutting tight turns.

Suddenly, I saw a snowboarder in all black gear come flying over the berm. He pulled a 360 and landed it like it was nothing.

"Nice," I whispered.

But he wasn't finished.

I had no idea how fast he was going, but he did a nose roll *then* a tail roll and the next thing I knew, he was doing the tightest switch Ollie I'd ever seen (live, anyway).

Man, he was good!

Within a few seconds, he was in line right behind me.

"Nice run," I said, my voice sounding younger than I wanted to.

He didn't say anything, but nodded.

It was my turn to get on the lift, and the guy in black ended up riding with me.

I glanced at him, but his lenses were tinted green and yellow, so I couldn't tell if he was even looking back at me.

Before I had a chance to say anything else, he pulled a pair of earbuds out of his pocket and stuck them in his ears. His music was so loud I could hear almost every word. I recognized the song, which was on the soundtrack to my favourite D-Day video. I listened to the drumbeat and remembered the image of him doing a front flip off some awesome mountain in Japan.

I poked him in the arm and he didn't move for about ten seconds. Then he slowly pulled out one earbud.

"Yeah?"

"That song. The one you're listening to? It's on D-Day's *Second Course* DVD. Have you seen it?"

I stared into the green-and-yellow lenses, but all I saw was my own goofy reflection.

"No," he finally said.

"You should. It's epic." My whole life was going to fall apart in the morning, but I still had a few more hours I could pretend it wasn't. So, I kept talking.

"There's this one part where he does a 720 and he looks like he's going to bite it, but he makes a save at the last second. It's probably the coolest trick on there." I paused, waiting for him to say something. "The DVD, I mean."

There was no response at all. Just those green lenses turned toward me.

"*Second Course*," I added, embarrassed. He still didn't speak, so I kept going. "It's not as good as Cody White's *Whiteout*, but it's still pretty cool. I mean . . . epic . . . or sick or whatever."

He stared for another few seconds, then asked, "Are you done?"

"Uh, yeah."

He nodded. "Good."

The rest of the ride up the mountain was dead silent.

CHAPTER FOUR

I spent the rest of the afternoon catching glimpses of the guy in black. He was a few chairs ahead of me on the lift a couple of times, and twice I saw the flash of the sun against his goggles when he made impossibly quick turns ahead of me on a black diamond run.

He was faster than anyone I'd ever seen in person and his tricks were sweet. I never saw the guy wipe out, and I never caught up with him.

After an hour or so, I checked the time, knowing I had to get home before Mom did.

But as soon as I walked in the door, I knew I was too late.

"Steven?" she said, appearing in the kitchen doorway with one hand on her hip.

"What are you doing here?" I asked, before I could stop myself.

"Wondering why you *aren't* here," she said, frowning as she looked me over from boot to hat. "I guess I don't need to ask where you've been."

"I was just—"

"Breaking the only house rule?" she snapped.

Uh-oh.

"Thomas was—"

"This isn't about Thomas."

"It kind of is, Mom. I was supposed to ride with him after school, but he went to that kid's house. You let him go." I tried not to make the last part sound like an accusation, but it kind of was.

"Steven, you *cannot* go up the mountain alone."

"I know, but I figured since it was still light out and—"

"You figured wrong," she said, through gritted teeth.

I needed to try another tactic, so I took a deep breath. "Look, Mom, I totally get why we're supposed to use the buddy system, but—"

"There's no but, Steven."

"I'm thirteen years old!"

"And?"

I stared at her. "And I've been dragged all over the country, starting over and over and over again. Snowboarding is the *one thing* that makes me feel at home and—"

"And you are *not allowed* to do it alone."

43

"I'm totally responsible, Mom."

"Not the point."

"You let Thomas—"

"I've already told you, this is not about Thomas."

I could tell by her tone that I wasn't going to get anywhere. "Fine. I'm sorry," I sighed.

"I appreciate that, but there will be a punishment coming your way. Dad and I will talk about it after dinner." She shook her head. "In the meantime, you're dripping all over the floor."

I looked down and saw that I was standing in a small but growing puddle. By the time I glanced up again to apologize, she was already back in the kitchen.

I cleaned up my mess and carried my gear upstairs, wishing I hadn't been in such a hurry to get on the mountain. Mom was right. Aside from me and Thomas getting our homework and minor chores done on time and not fighting with each other, the buddy system was the only real rule we had to follow.

And I'd broken it.

I knew that Mom and Dad weren't the strictest parents on earth, but that didn't mean they couldn't come up with a brutal punishment. What if they took away my board? Banned me from the mountain? Or worse?

Worse?

Never mind. There was nothing worse than no snowboarding.

Once my gear was back in the closet, I changed

into some sweats and flopped on my bed, wondering exactly how tough they would be.

I must have fallen asleep, because I didn't know Thomas was home until he swung open my door and demanded, "What are you *doing*?"

"Huh?" I mumbled, rubbing my eyes. "Crashing, I guess."

"No," he said, shaking his head like I was speaking another language. "I mean, what are you *doing*?"

I stretched and yawned, wondering why he was so worked up. "Waiting to find out what kind of punish—"

"I'm your brother, right?" he demanded.

Huh?

"Uh . . . yeah."

"Your blood brother."

"What?" I rubbed my eyes. "Yeah, obviously."

"So . . ." he paused, waiting for me to fill in the blank, but I had no idea what he was talking about. That is, until he said, "That means Cody White is *my* cousin, too, Steven."

Whoa!

That was enough to wake me up.

I sat up so quickly I was dizzy for a second. "I—"

"You couldn't give me a heads-up?" he asked, eyes wide. "You couldn't warn me that kids were going to be asking me all kinds of questions about my *famous cousin*?"

I felt the air leave my lungs. "Oh, man. You didn't say anything stupid, did you?"

He raised one eyebrow at me. "You mean something more stupid than what *you* said?"

Did he have to act so superior about it?

I wrapped my arms around my knees, feeling my whole body tense up. "Seriously, Thomas. Did you blow it?"

"Did *I*?" he choked. "Wait, are you really asking me if *I* blew it?" Before I could answer, he continued, "I heard you're bringing a gold medal to school tomorrow."

"Okay, the thing is—"

"From Powder Fest." He paused. "*You* are bringing a Powder Fest gold medal to school. Tomorrow."

"I guess," I said, shrugging as I felt a headache coming on.

"You guess?" He rolled his eyes. "Dude, why can't you just be normal, for once?"

"Thanks a lot."

"I mean it. All you had to do was walk into that school and act like a normal person. Why'd you have to make it so complicated?"

I told him the honest truth. "Because nobody cares about a normal person."

He stared at me. "How do you know?"

"Because I've been a total normal *nobody* at every school I've gone to. I wanted things to be different this time."

"Well, they're definitely different." He sighed. "A gold medal. How are you gonna pull that off?"

"I don't know. I'll figure something out," I said, my voice barely more than a whisper.

The expression on my face must have been pretty messed up, because Thomas started to look sorry for me instead of mad.

Why didn't he ever make the kind of stupid mistakes that I did?

He sat down on the end of my bed and was quiet for almost a whole minute before he finally said, "There's no way Dad would let you take a gold medal to school."

That was the least of my problems. "I don't even *have* one."

He shook his head. "What I'm saying is, if you *did* have one, Dad would keep it in a safe or something."

"Well, yeah. It would be worth a fortune."

"So?" he said, smiling at me.

"So, what?" I asked.

He sighed. "Do I really have to spell this out?"

"Apparently."

He rolled his eyes. "Just tell the kids at school that Dad wouldn't let you bring it in."

I opened my mouth, then closed it again when I realized the kid was a total genius. For the first time I could remember, I didn't mind that he was acting like a big brother, giving *me* advice. His plan would totally save me!

47

"That's so simple," I said, softly. "But so perfect. Of course Dad wouldn't let me take it to school."

"Exactly," Thomas said, nodding.

"Boys!" Mom called from downstairs. "Dinner!"

I high-fived my brother for the awesome idea and felt a huge weight drop off my shoulders as we ran downstairs.

But when I turned the corner and saw Dad sitting at the kitchen table, arms crossed and a stern expression on his face, I knew only half of my problems had been solved.

"Thomas," Dad said, reaching to ruffle my brother's hair when he sat down. Then he turned to me.

"Hi, Dad," I said, trying to smile. "How was work?"

"Fine." He cleared his throat. "Mom was just telling me about your solo trip up the mountain."

"Seriously?" Thomas gasped, then turned toward me, shaking his head. "*Wow*. Busy day, Steven."

"Yeah," I muttered.

"Not your best or brightest move, son," Dad said.

"I know. I'm sorry," I told him, bracing myself for bad news. How many days of boarding was I going to miss?

"You're on laundry, vacuum and garbage duty for the next two weeks."

"What?" I gasped, totally stunned.

"Laundry, vacuum—"

"No, I heard you." I paused. "I just thought you'd take away my board and—"

"Well, Mom and I are open to that, if you'd prefer—"

"No!" I yelped.

"Christmas vacation starts on Friday, and we know snowboarding will be a huge part of that," Mom said, pulling a roasted chicken out of the oven. "We want to punish you for what you did, not destroy your Christmas break."

"Thank you," I said, jumping up to hug Dad, then Mom.

"You're welcome," they said at the same time. Then Mom added, "Don't *ever* do it again."

"I won't," I promised, and totally meant it.

I spent the whole meal smiling.

Everything had worked out, for once. I wasn't going to miss a second of snowboarding *and* I had a foolproof plan to deal with my White Lie.

Life was perfect.

Or so I thought.

When my alarm went off the next morning, I didn't even hit the snooze bar. I jumped out of bed to head for the bathroom and almost ran right into Mom.

"You're up," she said, totally surprised.

"Yup."

"I was on my way to wake you."

"No need," I told her, humming as I walked toward the shower.

I heard her mumble something about wonders never ceasing as she started down the stairs.

I kept humming while I shampooed, soaped and rinsed myself off. By the time I headed back to my bedroom to get dressed, Thomas was rubbing his eyes in the bright lights of the hallway.

"You're up?" he asked.

"Yup," I told him, pushing my door open and heading straight for the closet.

I wasn't feeling nearly as much pressure to blend in as I had on my first day. I dug around until I found a clean white T-shirt, the bright green North Face hoodie I'd bought with my birthday money last year and some black cords. I stuck with the same Vans I'd worn the day before, not even caring that my feet would be soaked by the time I got to school.

By the time Thomas joined me at the breakfast table, I'd almost polished off my second waffle and was thinking about a third. But just as I lifted another delicious bite toward my mouth, the doorbell rang.

"Who could that be?" Mom asked, frowning.

"I'll find out," Thomas said, starting to stand up.

"No, you finish your breakfast," she told him, tightening the belt on her old bathrobe as she turned the corner.

I was too busy chewing to pay any attention to what was happening at the front door.

"Steven?" Mom called.

"Yeah?"

She reappeared with a confused look on her face. "Someone's here . . . for you."

"For me?" I asked, swallowing my mouthful.

"For him?" Thomas asked, looking as confused as Mom.

"Carlos?" Mom asked.

"Oh!" I said, grinning as my new friend came around the corner in a bright orange puffy jacket. "How's it going?"

"Good," he said, pulling his backpack strap onto his shoulder. "You ready to head out?"

"Sure," I said, grabbing the last piece of my waffle in one hand and my plate in the other.

"Where are you going?" Mom asked.

Was she kidding? "School."

"Oh, right. Of course," she said, laughing. "School."

I rinsed my plate and put it in the dishwasher, listening closely as Carlos introduced himself to Thomas, my genius brother, who had saved the day.

As they talked, it felt awesome to have a *friend* in my kitchen.

"See you later," I called over my shoulder as Carlos and I stepped onto the snow-packed front porch.

We walked down the driveway, snow crunching loudly under our feet, then turned toward the school. I couldn't help smiling to myself, happy that everything was turning out awesome in Oregon.

I had a *friend* and more of them were waiting for me at Evergreen. Popularity felt even better than I'd imagined.

"Is it in there?" Carlos suddenly asked, nodding toward my backpack.

"What?"

He looked at me like I was crazy. "The medal, dude."

"Oh," I mumbled, disappointed that he'd brought it up so soon. I'd expected to talk about other stuff too. "You mean the Powder Fest medal?"

"What, you have one from the X Games too?" he asked, chuckling.

"No," I said, trying to laugh along.

"So, can I see it?"

I cleared my throat. "Uh . . . my dad wouldn't let me bring it to school."

"Because it's too valuable?"

"Yeah," I agreed.

"Makes sense," he said, with a nod.

I breathed a sigh of relief and started to smile again. That was so easy!

"I can come over after school."

"Huh?"

"I can just see it at your place. Man, that's going to be so cool!"

"Yeah," I said, quietly.

How was I supposed to get out of that one?

I barely listened to Carlos the rest of the way to school. I was too busy trying to come up with a brilliant reason he couldn't come over to my house.

Ever.

And that was ridiculous! I finally had a friend and I couldn't hang out with him?

Of course, I had all day to come up with a plan.

When we walked through the main doors and into a crowd of noisy kids, Carlos said, "I'll save you a seat at lunch," then made a left turn down the hallway.

I kept my head down as I hustled over to my locker to dump my bag. I had to be ready for the questions that were going to fly at me in homeroom, and that meant staying calm.

My dad wouldn't let me bring it in. It's too valuable.

It's in a safe deposit box.

Cody would kill me if anything happened to it.

Oooh. I liked that one.

A few people said hi or nodded at me as I made my way to homeroom. I smiled back, like my brain wasn't going a thousand miles an hour. By the time I settled into a seat at the back, I could feel the sweat on the back of my neck.

You can do this. Just stay calm and stick with the simplest explanation.

My dad wouldn't let me.

No one could argue with that.

Someone poked me in the back, and I turned to see

the glitter girl from the day before. The nice one.

"Hey," I said, turning to smile at her.

"I'm Morgan," she announced. "I don't think I told you that yester—"

"Did you bring it?" a dark-haired boy in a Nike sweatshirt asked.

"Bring it?" I asked, as my palms started to sweat. "You mean the medal?"

"Yeah, let's see it," a couple of others chimed in.

The next thing I knew, I was surrounded by buzzing voices and hot breath. I started to feel a little claustrophobic and wished they weren't crowding me so much.

"Can I hold it?" a girl asked, leaning on the corner of my desk.

"Me first," someone whined from behind me.

"Give him some space, you guys," Glitter Morgan said, and I was grateful for the help.

A couple of kids stepped back, but they all continued to stare at me, like something awesome was about to happen.

I wished it was.

I took a deep breath and loudly told them, "I don't have it."

"I knew it," someone muttered, and the buzz in the air was replaced with groans and I-told-you-so's.

"No!" I practically shouted. "I mean, I *have* it, just not here."

"Why not?" the whiner asked.

"My dad says it's way too valuable to bring to school."

I crossed my fingers under the desk, waiting to see how they would react.

I saw at least three kids nod, and some murmured that their parents would probably say the same thing.

I was off the hook!

I leaned back in my seat, relief flowing through my blood, when I heard a familiar voice.

"You didn't bring the medal," Nolan said.

I felt my whole body tense up. "Uh, no. Because my dad—"

"It's cool," he said, raising a hand for me to stop talking. "I get it. The thing's probably worth major bucks, right?"

I nodded and repeated, "Yup. Major bucks."

To my huge relief, the room started to fill up with sound again. Someone pushed a desk into place and the metal legs rumbled against the floor. A bunch of pencils dropped on the floor. Two girls whispered and giggled at their secrets. A textbook was opened and pages rustled.

It was normal again.

I let out the breath I hadn't realized I was holding. Everything was going to be just fine. Thomas was my new hero.

I relaxed in my seat, feeling the solid comfort of the backrest against my shoulder blades.

Life was good.

That is, until Nolan dropped into the seat next to mine and gave me a strange look.

Uh-oh.

When he spoke his voice was the loudest sound in the room. "So, I was wondering . . ."

The whispering girls turned to look, along with everyone else who had walked away.

Everyone seemed to be waiting for him to finish asking his question, but he was totally silent, eyebrows raised, that strange look still on his face.

I heard the hands of the clock above Mrs. Hawthorne's desk ticking. I smelled the marker that one of the girls had been using on the whiteboard. I felt the anticipation in the room.

Even though every single part of my body told me not to do it, I finally broke the silence and asked, "Wondering what?"

Nolan smiled, and the back of my neck started to prickle with sweat.

"I was just wondering," he said, again, drawing out the words, "how exactly you're related."

"To Cody White?" I asked.

"Yeah."

I swallowed hard, my mind racing. Was it some kind of a trick? I'd already told Nolan and everyone else how we were related.

I took a breath, bracing myself. "Like I said before, he's my cousin."

I glanced from one face to the next and was relieved to see smiles.

That is, until Nolan asked, "On what side?"

"What?" I asked, turning to stare at him.

"On what side?" he repeated, a gleam in his eye. "Like, are your dad and his mom brother and sister?"

"Uh—"

"Or are you related on your mom's side?"

I'd read enough about Cody White to know he had two sisters called Ashley and Kirsten and that he was the middle kid. I knew his dad, Kirk, used to be totally into surfing and his mom, Laura, came from a softball family.

But did his *parents* have brothers and sisters?

I tried to think back to every scrap of information I'd read about that family, but it was hard to do while everyone was staring at me.

I felt a sinking sensation, deep in my stomach.

Should I be related to Cody White through my mom or my dad?

I had no idea.

"I . . . uh—"

"It's a pretty simple question," Nolan said, obviously thrilled about putting me on the spot.

"It's just . . . I, uh . . ."

"See?" Nolan shouted to the crowd, triumphantly. "I *told you* he was a liar!"

CHAPTER FIVE

All of the kids stared at me and I felt total panic racing through my veins. It wasn't just my neck sweating anymore. My hands and armpits had joined in. In fact, my whole body felt sticky and hot, like I was wearing all of my snowboarding gear in the middle of August.

"I was just—" I began, but had no idea where the sentence should go from there.

Mostly because Nolan was right.

I *was* a liar.

It wasn't a mean or dangerous lie. I hadn't done it to hurt anybody. All I'd wanted to do was fit in, for once.

"I only—" I began again, but the words just dangled in the air.

There was nothing I could say, so I said . . . nothing.

And the rest of the kids didn't say anything to me,

either. They just took a step or two back, whispered to each other and stared, like I was part of a zoo exhibit. And not even a good one. More like a petting zoo.

I was like the goat that tried to chew on their shoelaces.

Eventually, a couple of people wandered away, but a few stayed to stare at me while I tried to look busy. I did my best to ignore them, unzipping my backpack and digging around, searching for . . . nothing. Well, some pride maybe. I pushed past the loose ballpoint pens and a couple of textbooks. Even though it was one hundred percent impossible, I couldn't help wishing that by some kind of miracle, I'd find a Powder Fest gold medal underneath all of my junk.

But of course I didn't.

When Mrs. Hawthorne entered the room, I sat up straight and stared directly at her, pretending I didn't notice the pointing fingers or hear the snickers.

But *she* noticed.

"What's going on in here, Room Seven Twenty-Four?"

Heads swivelled back and forth, eyes darting around to see who would tell her, but no one spoke up.

Mrs. Hawthorne made eye contact with practically every kid in the room, squinting at some and shooting laser beam stares at others, but she barely glanced at me.

Sighing, she ran through the attendance list, only

frowning slightly when she called my name and a couple of people giggled.

By the time homeroom was over, I couldn't wait to get out into the hallway where I hoped I'd disappear into the crowd.

Unfortunately, the story of my White Lie seemed to be moving down the hallway a few feet in front of me. Every few steps, someone turned to stare at me, some laughing and others shaking their heads.

I tried to keep my arms tight at my sides and hunch my shoulders so I'd be as close to invisible as possible. But invisible wasn't going to happen.

I got bumped, elbowed and almost tripped (which I was pretty sure was an accident) on the way to my Science class, but I managed to make it there on time and in one piece.

Unfortunately, it turned out that we were supposed to partner off. It was no surprise when I ended up being the odd man out, but that didn't make it any less embarrassing. To make matters worse, instead of turning one of the twosomes into a threesome, Mr. McDowell made me be *his* partner.

It had to be the worst idea ever and I spent almost a whole hour standing at the front of the room while the whispering continued.

My next class was no better, and by the time noon rolled around, I was more than ready to go home and never come back.

I knew lunchtime would be worse than my classes and wished the bell would never ring.

But it did.

I dropped my books off at my locker and grabbed my lunch from the top shelf. Taking a deep breath, I joined the stream of kids on the way to the cafeteria, dreading my arrival with every step.

But when I walked into a room jam-packed with kids, one of the first things I saw was a familiar orange jacket.

Carlos.

When we'd split up that morning, he'd promised to save me a seat!

Glad I didn't have to wait in line for a hot lunch and risk the chance of missing him, I hurried through the crowd.

Instead of searching for an empty space next to a bunch of strangers, I had a seat to fill. A spot of my own, being saved by a skateboarder named Carlos. It didn't matter how many kids thought I was a liar or a loser (or both), I still had a friend.

Smiling, I arrived at his table and started to sit down across from him.

"Hey," I said. "How's it—"

"Whoa!" Carlos barked, holding one hand up to stop me. "What are you doing?"

I stared at him, confused. "Eating lunch? With you?"

"Uh, Steven—"

Most of the kids were seated, but I was still standing. All I wanted to do was slip into my spot and blend in.

"You said you were going to save me a seat," I reminded him.

"Shh." He glanced from one side to the other, obviously hoping no one had heard me.

But everyone was listening.

"This morning, Carlos," I said, hearing a crack in my voice. "When we got to school. *You said*—"

"You lied about being Cody White's cousin."

I could feel my cheeks turning red. How did news spread so fast in this place?

"I know, but—"

"And you invited me over to see his medal."

"Well, actually you kind of invited yourself," I began, but when I saw the angry look on his face, I stopped talking.

"Why did you lie to me?" he demanded.

"I thought—"

His voice dropped down to a whisper. "Were you trying to make me look stupid?"

"No!" I yelped, shaking my head. "No way. Look, I—"

"Find another seat, Steven," he said, turning his attention to his wrinkled brown lunch bag.

"But—"

"Seriously, man. Get out of here."

I could feel a thousand eyes on me, and my face

burned with shame as I stepped away from the table.

I glanced around the room, hoping for a sympathetic look, but the other students' faces were a blur. And when I couldn't make out the letters of the lunch specials on the chalkboard sign, I knew I was dangerously close to crying.

I wasn't going to do that in front of the whole school. *No way.*

I started moving toward the doorway and all I could hear were words like "weirdo" and "liar."

I made it out to the hall, but had no idea where I could eat my lunch in private. I hurried toward the school's main entrance, just wanting to get out of the building.

Then I slowed down. If I went home, Mom would ask me a thousand questions I didn't want to answer. I didn't want her and Dad to know anything about the White Lie *or* the disaster it had turned into.

I couldn't believe what a mess I'd made of everything.

For once, I'd made my first friend in just a couple of days. And even better? I was instantly popular with a bunch more people. But I'd blown it.

And I'd blown it in less than twenty-four hours.

I opened one of the doors that led to the furnace room and let it close behind me with a loud bang.

It was darker than the hallway, but the flickering fluorescent light was enough for me to see that I'd ended up in an empty concrete stairway that smelled like cleaning fluids and old milk.

Sighing, I sat on the top step and opened my lunch bag. Inside were an egg salad sandwich and some carrot sticks.

Just when I thought the day couldn't get any worse.

Once my sandwich was unwrapped and I'd taken my first soggy bite, I closed my eyes and wished I was up on the mountain, spraying fresh powder with every sharp turn of my board.

I took another bite, pretending my sad sandwich was a big, juicy steak I was eating to celebrate a huge win at Mammoth. I pictured a table filled with snowboarding legends. Matty Doakes, dipping a lobster claw into melted butter. Vigo, working on a grilled lamb chop. Cody White . . . well, I didn't want to think about Cody White.

The sound of my chewing and swallowing was the only noise in the stairway until the door suddenly swung open.

"What are you doing in here?" a small man with a booming voice demanded. He had a broom in one hand and a garbage can in the other.

"Eating my lunch?" I said, hopefully.

He shook his head. "You can't eat in here."

"It's fine," I assured him. "It's more comfortable than you'd think and—"

"This is a fire exit," he interrupted, pointing to the sign above the door.

Come on. Couldn't one single thing go my way?

"I can't just stay in here until lunch is over?" I begged.

He actually looked sorry for me and I thought he was going to give me a break. But then he shook his head slowly and said, "No."

Sighing, I gathered my stuff together and trudged back into the hallway. I wasn't about to eat my lunch in the bathroom, so I headed for my locker and sat on the floor in front of it.

Checking the wall clock, I realized that the worst day of my life was only half over.

Walking home alone that afternoon, I had plenty of time to think. I still had three whole days to get through before Christmas break. That seemed like forever, but it wasn't enough time to make anyone forget or for me to make some friends. That meant I'd be spending the whole two weeks off alone. After all, Thomas would be too busy hanging out with his new buddies to bother with me.

"There he is," some kid said, as I turned onto my street. "The wannabe."

I couldn't decide if that was better or worse than being called "the liar."

When I got home, Thomas was on his way out the door.

"Where are you going?"

"Matt's house," he replied.

Like I had any idea who Matt was.

"What happened to Ben?" I asked, thinking of yesterday's new friend. I couldn't help hoping Ben had ditched Thomas as quickly as Carlos ditched me.

"He's coming too. So's Dylan."

"Have fun," I muttered, stepping past him and into the hallway.

"What's your problem?" he asked.

"Nothing." *Everything.*

"Hold on." He followed me back inside. "When you left here this morning, you were set. I gave you a solid plan."

"Not solid enough."

He stared at me. "What's that supposed to mean? What happened?"

"Don't you have a video game to play somewhere?"

He frowned. "It can wait."

"Yeah, right." As if I could ever be more important than killing zombies.

"I'm serious," my little brother said. "I want to know what happened."

"I blew it, okay?"

He folded his arms. "Impossible. All you had to say was that Dad wouldn't let you bring the medal to school."

"That's what I thought," I said, groaning.

"Just tell me, Steven."

So I did. I flopped on the couch and told him the whole horrible story. I didn't even look at his face until I was finished.

"So," I said, shrugging. "That's what happened."

Thomas shook his head. "Why didn't you just say that our dads are brothers?"

Hadn't he listened to a word I'd said?

"Because I don't *know* whether Cody White's dad has any brothers, Thomas! I mean, there's nothing in the articles or books I've read that say anything about—"

"Dude, that's the *only* way we'd have the same last name."

"What?"

"Both of our dads are Whites," he explained. "If our moms were sisters, they'd have different last names. Same thing if it was our mom and his dad who were brother and sister, or the other way around."

I felt all of the energy ooze out of my body, like slime. I closed my eyes, exhausted by my own stupidity.

Why, why, *why* hadn't I thought of that?

"Steven?" Thomas asked worriedly. "Are you okay?"

I shook my head, amazed that I'd made every possible wrong move. It was like the last Winter X Games, when D-Day tried to pull a brand new trick called a Locust 1080. It would have been epic and the medal would have been his for sure, but he didn't have enough speed going into it. He tried to correct himself in mid-air, *then* blew the landing. After that, he disappeared and no one had seen him since. It was exactly what I would have liked to do.

Disappear. *Forever.*

I groaned. "This is a total disaster."

"It's not *that* bad," Thomas lied.

"Are you joking?"

"Well, maybe the kids will forget the whole thing over Christmas break."

I stared at him. "Would you?"

"Probably not," he admitted, quietly.

"I hate this place," I told him, and I meant it. "I hate everything about it."

He raised one eyebrow, then grabbed my arm to pull me off the couch and over to the window.

All I could see was the mountain, covered in fresh, crunchy snow and practically glowing against the bright blue sky.

It was beautiful.

"Really?" Thomas asked. "You hate *everything* about this place?"

I sighed. "I like the mountain."

"Then let's go." He yanked on my arm again, this time pulling me toward the stairs. "Get your gear."

"I thought you were going to Mark's house."

"Matt's, and I'll call to let him know something came up."

"You don't have to do this," I said, quietly.

"Yes I do. We have a buddy system, remember? If I don't go, you *can't* go," he reminded me.

"I know, but—"

"And if we don't go, all you're going to do is mope around the house."

"I'm just saying—"

Thomas rolled his eyes. "Quit trying to talk me out of it, man."

So I quit trying and ran upstairs to get my stuff.

Once we were on the lift, I could almost forget exactly how bad my day had been. For the next couple of hours I could focus on something I loved instead.

I saw a black jacket a couple of chairs ahead of us, but I couldn't tell if it was the guy I'd seen the day before. The guy who was an awesome snowboarder . . . and not much of a talker.

Thomas and I didn't say anything on the way up, but it wasn't awkward or weird. I found myself wishing we hung out together more often, like we did when we were little. We used to be totally inseparable, but once he got into video games and I got serious about snowboarding, it was like we didn't have anything in common anymore.

I glanced at Thomas, still surprised that he'd given up an afternoon of gaming with new friends to hang with me.

"Want to do Crystal Bowl?" he asked, looking at the map of runs when we got off the chairlift. "Or maybe Meadow Loop?"

I shook my head. "Nah. Let's try Crackerjack."

Thomas smiled. "Whatever you say, big brother."

We adjusted our goggles, strapped on our boards and we were off.

I quickly realized that it was pretty sweet being out on the mountain with Thomas. We may not have hung out much lately, but everything felt really natural on our boards. Maybe it was because of those old inseparable days, but neither of us ever had to think about what the other guy was doing. We took turns leading and tried to outdo each other with jumps. I pulled a 180, then slowed down to watch him wipe out when he tried to land a 360 behind me.

"Almost," I told him, grinning. He could beat me at a few things, but snowboarding wasn't one of them.

We rode the lift back up and decided to do Crackerjack again as we neared the top.

I saw a couple of kids I recognized from that disaster in the cafeteria. Hoping for the best, I started to wave, but they snickered and turned away from me.

Whatever. I was having fun with my brother, anyway.

All the way down, Thomas and I did tricks and caught serious air. We wiped out, laughed, and got up to do it again.

I was shaking out my goggles when a flash of black

whipped past me. I stopped what I was doing and stared as the guy worked his way down the run, catching air in the gnarliest places and landing like it was nothing.

I didn't hear Thomas stop next to me.

"What's going on?" he asked.

"That guy," I said, pointing. "Does he seem familiar to you?"

Thomas turned to look and nodded. "I might have seen him on the lift."

"No, I mean his style. He rides like someone we know."

"No." Thomas shook his head. "He *shreds*. I don't know anyone who can do that."

I watched the black figure turn into a speck, then disappear around a corner.

For the rest of the afternoon, I kept my eyes peeled for him, hoping to get another look at how he rode.

But I didn't see him again.

CHAPTER SIX

The last three days of school before the break felt like three whole years.

The kids eventually stopped pointing and whispering, but what they did next was worse. They completely ignored me. I was like a ghost, floating down the hallways and sitting through classes while no one said a word to me.

And I mean *no one*.

I ate lunch wherever I could find a private spot, even ending up outside near the garbage cans on Wednesday. I'm not sure whether the cold was worse than the loneliness, but they were both pretty bad.

On Thursday, the wind was pretty nasty, so I sat in a little alcove by the gymnasium and opened up my lunch bag.

When I was halfway through my peanut butter

sandwich, the janitor, whose name I'd learned was James, peeked around the corner.

"Everything okay in there?" he asked.

I swallowed a bite of my sandwich. "Yeah."

"Okay, then," he said, and started to walk away.

"Wait!" I called after him. I was desperate to talk to anyone, even an adult, so I dug around in my bag until I found the chocolate chip walnut cookies Mom had baked. They were my absolute favourite, and I'd been saving them for last, but a bit of company would be worth it.

"Cookies?" I asked, offering the baggie to James.

"You don't like them?" he asked, obviously surprised.

"They're awesome, but you can have them," I told him, scooting over so he could sit down.

"Thank you very much," he said. He grabbed a cookie and walked away, eating it.

Another failed plan.

Alone again, I slumped back against the wall, wondering when my luck would finally change.

When I'd finished my sandwich, I headed back to my locker. On the way, I passed Ethan, who was racing toward the auditorium with some sheet music in his hands.

"The big concert's tomorrow!" he crowed, like it was the best news on earth. "See you there!"

"Sure," I muttered. The concert was just another chance for me to sit alone while everyone around me had fun together. I could do *that* anywhere.

I sat on the floor in front of my locker to wait for the longest lunch period ever to come to an end. It seemed like each day that forty-five minutes stretched a little more.

My new *Air* magazine had arrived, so I flipped to the table of contents. The issue featured an interview with Tall Paul Hogarth, who had killed at Mammoth, as well as a photo spread on Chun Dahn, who was one of the best Big Air competitors at the last Winter X Games. He'd managed to pull off the sweetest tricks ever about ten minutes before D-Day choked on that Locust 1080. It was a classic case of the best and worst moments in sports colliding.

If I was a pro, I'd be at the top of the game all the time. No matter what.

And maybe I'd be sponsored by Burton or some other company, so I'd never have to worry about buying another board. They'd beg me to ride the Green Beast I wanted so badly. Or maybe they'd design a special Steven White limited-edition board.

That would be seriously awesome.

"Hey, Steven," Glitter Morgan said, as she walked by with a couple of other girls.

I kind of grunted back, thinking she might be making fun of me.

I tried to slip back into my pro daydream, but the bell rang.

On Friday, the hallways were buzzing with excitement about the Christmas concert all morning. I knew the whole school would be there, so the auditorium would be packed. The last thing I wanted to do was beg for a seat.

When it was time for my English class to walk down the hallway, single file, I darted out of line and headed for the nurse's office.

"Steven!" Ethan called, then hurried to catch up with me. "The concert's that way." He pointed down the hall.

"I have a stomach ache," I told him.

"You're going to miss it?"

I nodded. "I'll catch it next year," I said, hoping my family would be thousands of miles away from Timber by then.

"Oh," he said, looking disappointed. "Well, I hope you feel better."

"Thanks," I said, knowing I'd be feeling just fine once I was safely settled in the nurse's office.

When the final bell rang to end the day, I hurried back to my locker to grab my stuff. Everyone was shouting and laughing as they made their way to the main doors.

No one even wished me a Merry Christmas.

Well, Mrs. Hawthorne did, but she said it to everyone.

And Glitter Morgan smiled and waved, but I couldn't

tell if she was being sarcastic, so it didn't really count.

On the walk home, Carlos was only about twenty feet ahead of me, so I took a deep breath and called his name.

When he turned around, he didn't say anything, but he stood still long enough for me to catch up.

"Hey," I said, nodding at him. "Maybe I'll see you around over the break."

"Maybe," he said, without much enthusiasm.

Still, it was better than being told to drop dead or hearing the word liar for the eight millionth time.

I cleared my throat. "Well, if I don't see you beforehand, have a good Christmas."

"Yeah." He nodded and started to walk away, but stopped after a few steps. "You too," he said, barely loud enough for me to hear.

"Thanks."

He obviously didn't want to walk with me, so I slowed down to give him some space.

Of course, Carlos was only one small part of my very big problem, and I spent the rest of the walk home trying to figure out a way to turn things around at school. The good part was that I had a couple of weeks to brainstorm. And maybe that *was* enough time for some of the kids to forget about my White Lie.

Yeah, right.

Nobody would forget about it.

I started daydreaming about how cool it would be if

I told Cody White what had happened and he jumped on a plane to Oregon to help me out. What if he went to school with me? I smiled as I pictured the expression on everyone's faces as we cruised through the hallway, laughing and joking.

It would be sweet!

At dinner that night, Mom passed me a bowl of salad and asked, "So, how was the last day of school?"

"Uh," I mumbled, reaching for the dressing and turning the bottle over to read the ingredients, *as if I cared*. I was a terrible liar (something I'd proven to Evergreen's entire student body already), but I didn't want to tell my parents the truth, either. Mom had looked so happy when Carlos showed up at the house that one morning.

I didn't want to disappoint her.

"Steven?" Dad said, looking worried.

"It was good," Thomas interrupted. "But not as good as Christmas vacation, right Steven?"

"Definitely," I said, grateful for the help.

"So, what do you boys feel like doing with all this spare time?" Dad asked.

"Aside from getting your rooms organized and helping with some of the other unpacking," Mom added.

I shrugged. "I don't know. Do some snowboarding, if Thomas wants to go with me."

"I've actually got tomorrow off," Dad said. "We could all go."

"Really?" I gasped, excitement running through me for the first time in days. "That would be awesome!"

"Great," he said, spooning some sunflower seeds onto his salad. "Are you in, honey?"

Mom laughed. "Maybe later in the season. I'm going to be spending the day polishing my resumé."

"Thomas?" Dad asked.

My brother shook his head. "I'm hanging with Brian tomorrow."

As if any of us knew who *that* was.

"Another time, then," Dad said, then smiled at me. "I guess it's just us, buddy."

"Sweet!"

"Provided you get your chores out of the way tonight," Mom said. "I don't think the vacuum has been out of the cupboard since Dad and I decided on your punishment."

"I'll do it right now."

"And I think we're ready for a couple of loads of wash," Dad added.

"No problem," I told them, with a quick nod. "I'm on it."

It was still dark when Dad and I got up the next morning and we crept around the house so we wouldn't wake the others up. After we'd both showered and dressed, I poured the cereal while Dad filled his pack with a couple of sandwiches, snacks and drinks.

It had been a long time since we'd done something together, just the two of us, and I was pretty excited to have him to myself for the whole day. I couldn't wait to show him some of the tricks I'd been working on, knowing he'd be impressed.

And he was!

"What do you call that?" he asked on the way down Lost Loop.

"A Chicken Salad," I told him.

He grinned. "Are you kidding?"

"No," I said, laughing. "That's what it's called."

It was kind of difficult to grab the heelside of the board by reaching my front hand between my feet, mostly because I needed some extra airtime. But I was getting pretty good at it.

"Who comes up with these names?" Dad asked, shaking his head.

"I don't know, but if I'd gripped the board with my back hand, it would be a Roast Beef."

"Wow," he said, chuckling.

"And if I did a Roast Beef and a Nose Grab at the same time, you know what they'd call it?"

"A Tuna Sandwich?" Dad suggested. "Or maybe a Banana Split?"

"A Rusty Trombone," I told him.

"Of course! The old Rusty Trombone," he said, pretending to smack his forehead. "How could I forget?"

"Very funny," I said, my laugh turning into a snort.

"You know, I remember when it took total concentration for you just to stay on your feet. You must have been five or six when we first took you out. And now you're mastering tricks."

I remembered the video I'd seen on YouTube of Cody White when he was twelve. Just a year younger than me and he was doing full-on flips and jumping off cliffs.

I could only dream of doing a flip.

"Show me something else on the next berm," Dad said, taking off ahead of me to get a good view.

As I pushed off, a whole bunch of tricks zipped through my head and I finally settled on one that was pretty easy but looked cool and difficult.

I'd been down Lost Loop a few times during my visits to the mountain, and I knew the perfect jump was just a little farther down the hill.

I built up speed so I could get a nice launch, bending my knees and shifting my weight to get the most out of the board.

The jump was close and I took a breath before I popped off of it. As I sailed through the air, I grabbed the board's nose with my right hand, then reached back as far as I could with my left, to grab the tail. It was amazing to think my arms hadn't been long enough to do it just a year ago.

I let go of both ends and straightened up just before I landed a little harder than I wanted to.

"You okay?" Dad asked, when he saw me rubbing my knee.

"Yup." Before he got too sidetracked by the rough landing, I told him, "That's called a Cannonball."

"I can see why."

"And some people call it a UFO."

"I like Cannonball," he said. "Nice job, Steven. Are you sure you're okay?"

"Definitely," I told him, starting to race ahead. "See you at the bottom!"

I wasn't allowed to wear headphones because my parents thought it was dangerous, but I could still hear my very own mental soundtrack as I made my way down the hill.

I liked to imagine there was a camera guy filming every jump and turn for an awesome video I hadn't given a title yet.

Dad and I waited in lift lines that got a little longer after every run, but I didn't mind. It was fun to hang out with him, even if we were just standing and waiting.

I even managed to ignore the looks I got whenever we ran into kids from school. And they seemed to be everywhere.

I was having a great day, but when we were riding up the mountain for the tenth or eleventh time, I heard the buzz of Dad's phone. I assumed it was Mom, but it didn't take long for me to realize it was someone else.

"Absolutely," Dad said. "I can be there at . . ." he pulled up his sleeve to check his watch, "two o'clock."

"Two o'clock *today*?" I whispered, hoping I was wrong.

Dad lifted a "hold on" finger at me and continued, "It's no problem, Jerry. You can count on me."

He'd barely hung up when I asked what was going on.

"That was Jerry, from work. His daughter was in a car accident and he needs to be with her. I told him I'd cover."

"But—"

He gave me a long look. "If you were in the hospital, you'd want me to be there, wouldn't you?"

"Yes," I admitted. But *I* wasn't in an accident, and the only place I wanted him to be was right here with me, on the mountain.

He nudged me with his elbow. "We'll have a chance to do this again. At least we got a few runs in, right?"

I nodded, but I wasn't ready to call it a day.

"Dad?"

"Yes?"

"Do you think I could maybe stay?"

"Stay? Here, you mean?"

"Yeah. Just for a couple more hours? I want to work on my Cross Rocket."

"Today?" Dad asked.

"Today," I said, nodding. "I'm *so* close."

Dad was quiet, thinking about it. "I don't know, Steven."

"You could leave your cellphone with me," I said, hopefully. "Then Mom wouldn't have to worry."

"I don't think that's a good idea," he said. "Sorry, bud."

"Dad, I'm thirteen now. That's old enough to *baby-sit* other kids. It should be old enough to look after myself." I took a breath. "Don't you think?"

He was quiet again, and as much as I wanted to say something else to try to convince him, I kept my mouth shut.

Finally, when we were almost ready to get off the lift, he said, "Okay. We'll try this out."

"Really?" I asked, totally surprised and excited.

"You have to be home by six o'clock. That means at the front door on the dot of six o'clock."

That wasn't much time! "You know, they have night skiing, Dad. It would be pretty awesome to board under the lights and—"

"Dinner is at six-thirty," he interrupted. "We don't live by the ski schedule. We live by . . ."

"Mom's," I finished for him.

"Well, the *family's* schedule is what I was going for."

"I get it," I said, feeling a little disappointed.

"Hey, it gets dark early, anyway. The lights will probably be on by four-thirty." He paused. "So, do we have a deal?"

Night boarding would have been sweet, but hanging out on my own for the afternoon was still pretty cool.

"Definitely," I promised, grinning.

"Good. I'll call Mom to let her know the plan when we finish this run."

"Sweet."

"And Steven?"

"Yeah?"

"I'm dead serious about six o'clock."

"Gotcha," I told him. I'd be there five minutes early, just to be on the safe side. "Thanks, Dad."

We chose Flying Squirrel for our final run and it turned out to be pretty fast and gnarly. I was concentrating too hard on tight turns and sudden jumps to hear a mental soundtrack, and when we got to the bottom, I was actually out of breath.

"Wow," Dad said, shaking his head. "That was pretty hairy."

I couldn't wait to do it again!

I hugged him goodbye and promised *again* to be home by six.

Waiting for the lift by myself wasn't as fun as hanging out with Dad, but the line moved pretty fast. Soon enough, my feet were dangling in mid-air halfway to the top.

That's when I saw that familiar black jacket and, when the guy turned to one side, a flash of green goggles.

This time, I would follow him and see if I could pick up any of his moves.

Lucky for me, he chose Flying Squirrel and I hurried to catch up with him.

He was moving really fast and catching air all over the place, but I did my best to keep an eye on him. Luckily, there weren't many people on the run, so it was pretty smooth sailing for me.

That is, until the guy in black turned a corner and I followed, faster than I should have.

I had no plans to hit a jump, and didn't even see it coming, but the next thing I knew, I was shooting through the air. I was out of control and had no way of slowing down when I spotted someone right in front of me.

It was too late to shout a warning and the only sound that came out of me was a squeak, right before I crashed into him.

Dazed, I lay in the snow for a few seconds, wondering how I'd ended up on my back.

"What was *that*?" an angry voice demanded.

I propped myself up on an elbow and saw that the voice belonged to the guy in black. He was on the ground too.

"Sorry," I offered, sliding my boots out of their

bindings so I could stand up. "I couldn't see."

"Obviously," he snorted.

I reached out to give him a hand getting up. He ignored it and pushed himself to his feet in one fluid motion.

I cleared my throat. "Are you okay?"

"Yeah, but my goggles are toast," he answered, pointing one gloved finger at the cracked green plastic.

I was too busy staring at his face to pay attention.

Rushing through my mind were a bunch of magazine covers, TV clips and the posters on my very own bedroom wall, but it still took me a few seconds to recognize the guy in front of me.

And when I did recognize him, it took me another second to realize what I'd done.

I'd plowed right into D-Day.

CHAPTER SEVEN

I stood and stared at one of my all-time greatest snow-boarding heroes, totally stunned that he was right in front of me.

Right in front of me!

I mean, I had posters of the guy on my *wall*. A T-shirt with his name on it. I'd watched his videos so many times, his tricks were practically burned onto my eyelids.

And he was a couple of feet away!

Danny Day, a sixteen-year-old pro, live and in person.

I felt my mouth hanging open and quickly shut it.

I'd been glued to the screen when he blew everyone away with awesome runs at Mammoth. And Whistler? I'd barely left the living room during the final round.

That's why his boarding style looked so familiar to

me. I'd been studying the guy's moves forever.

I swallowed hard as the truth hit me again.

D-Day was right in front of me!

Staring at me.

"Are you hurt or something?" he asked, his anger turning to concern.

I swallowed again, making a loud gulping noise. How long had I been staring at him like a fish gasping for air?

"Hello?" he said, waving one hand at me. "Are you okay?"

I cleared my throat. "I'm . . . uh . . . I'm fine."

The truth is, I was better than fine. *Way better.* I was awesome! I was talking to Danny Day! Well, staring at him, anyway.

There were so many images flashing through my head, I couldn't even identify them all. D-Day, soaring through the air on a 720. Gazing out from the cover of *Boarder*. Posing for an *Airway* catalogue. Standing on the podium next to Cody White!

Standing right in front of me.

"Are you sure?" he asked, doubtfully. "You look kind of—"

"Yeah!" I choked. "Yeah, I'm totally okay."

"Cool," he said, turning away like the conversation was over.

But it had barely started! I had so many questions to ask him, like what he was doing on my mountain and how long he'd be in town for. Was he training to make a comeback at the X Games in January? Just hanging out? Looking for someone to ride with? Oh, and I wanted to make sure I got a selfie with him on Dad's phone. That would show everyone at school, for sure!

But only if he stuck around long enough to pose for it.

"I'm Steven," I blurted at his back.

He turned around and saw my hand, stuck out for him to shake. Instead of reaching for it, he stared at it. *Forever.*

Finally, when my hand had been hanging long enough to create the weirdest and most awkward moment ever, he sighed and shook it.

"I'm . . . Derek," he said, quietly.

"I know . . ." I stopped. What? No, he was Danny. Danny Day. D-Day. What the heck? "Hold on . . . did you say *Derek*?"

He nodded, but didn't make eye contact. "Yeah." He paused for another couple of seconds before saying, "Derek Jones."

Derek Jones?

What was happening?

"Nice to meet you," I mumbled, totally confused.

I was more than a hundred percent sure that I was staring at D-Day. I would have bet my board on it. But to be even more sure, I studied his face more closely.

Yup.

There was the leftover bump from his broken nose at Whistler. The scar on his chin from a brutal crash in Japan. The brown eyes that were so dark they looked almost black in photos.

There was absolutely no doubt in my mind that I was standing in front of D-Day.

Did he really think I didn't recognize him?

It had to be a joke.

I looked past him, trying to spot a TV crew for a hidden camera show, but all I saw were other skiers and snowboarders enjoying an afternoon on the mountain.

He glanced over his shoulder to see what I was looking at, then frowned. "Are you sure you're okay?"

"Definitely," I said, my brain swirling with confusion. "*Derek.*"

"Okay," he said, squinting at me. Then he studied his cracked goggles again. "Well, it looks like I'm done, anyway."

What?

"No!" I gasped.

"Excuse me?" he said, one eyebrow raised.

"No! I mean, you can't leave." Not before I got my photo and talked to him about the X Games and . . . wait, I couldn't do any of that unless I called him out and made him admit he was D-Day.

Hold on.

I wanted him to *admit it*, when anyone else on the mountain would have been bragging about it?

That didn't make any sense!

He stared at me for what felt like a very long couple of seconds. "Exactly how weird is this going to get?"

"Weird?" I asked. I guess the whole conversation had been a little weird. Okay, *a lot* weird.

He nodded. "See ya."

Then he started to walk away again!

"Hold on," I begged, yanking my backpack off and unzipping it. "I have another pair in here," I muttered as I dug past granola bars and extra gloves. "Goggles, I mean." Why had I packed so much junk? There was no way I could eat that many graham crackers plus all the food Dad had thrown into his pack. And how did a pair of socks end up in there? When had I ever *changed my socks* while snowboarding? I shoved them aside, hearing the graham crackers break in their Ziploc bags.

"Look, I gotta go," D-Day said.

"Here!" I shouted, pulling the goggles free, along with a bunch of crumbs and bits of dirt. "You can borrow them," I told him, dangling my old Oakleys from my fingertips.

D-Day reached for them, then shook his head and dropped his hand like the goggles were covered in boogers or something even worse. "Nah."

"There's nothing wrong with them," I promised. "They're just old."

He still looked doubtful. "Thanks, but I shouldn't."

Shouldn't?

I wasn't going to let the moment end that quickly.

"Seriously," I told him, still offering the goggles, "it would be crazy to cut out early when the snow's this good."

He looked back up at the run behind us, where skiers and snowboarders were whipping through the air.

"It's supposed to rain tomorrow," I told him, even though I had no idea what the weatherman had predicted. "This could be the last good day in a while."

He looked up at the sky, then back at me and slowly nodded. "I guess."

I tried not to freak out, which was a lot tougher than it sounds.

He sighed, but finally took the goggles and slipped them on.

I hated to admit it, but they looked about ten times cooler on him than they did on me. In fact, I was pretty sure he was wearing the exact same pair on the cover of a *Blizzard* magazine in my stack at home.

Why hadn't I packed *that* in my bag? I could have asked him to sign it, right then and there. If I had a felt pen, he could've even signed the goggles when we were finished, so I could keep them as a souvenir. Come to think of it, I should have been carrying magazines and Sharpies with me whenever I was on the mountain, just in case.

I was missing what might be my only chance at an autograph because my pack was filled with socks!

Then again, he probably wouldn't sign anything if he was calling himself Derek Jones.

Danny Day.

I knew it was weird and I should totally stop, but I kept staring at him, amazed that I was only a couple of feet away from a total *legend*. A legend pretending to be someone else.

Pretending to be a nobody.

If someone had told me five years, five weeks or even five minutes ago that I'd be in this situation, I would have thought they were totally crazy.

But there I was, watching D-Day adjust *my* goggles.

It was awesome! Except for the whole name thing, anyway. Why the heck was he calling himself Derek?

Then again, did it really matter?

I knew who he was.

And I was about to go snowboarding with a world champion. Me and D-Day, hauling down runs at lightning speed and high-fiving at the bottom.

I couldn't wait to get started!

"So," I said, slipping my pack back onto my shoulders. "Let's roll."

"What?" D-Day said, sounding surprised.

"Let's roll," I repeated, slowly. That saying wasn't just a Kansas thing, was it? I mean, didn't they use it everywhere? "You know, let's get going."

He tilted his head like I was crazy. "I know what it *means.*"

"So, let's do this," I said, grinning.

"Us?" he said, like one of us had some super gross contagious disease.

Probably me.

"Yeah," I told him. "Us."

Obviously.

"Like, together?" He frowned.

"Not on the same board or anything, but yeah." I nodded. "Together."

He looked up the mountain like there was an answer up there somewhere. "I don't know."

"Don't know what?" I asked.

Was it because I was younger than him? Was sixteen really that much cooler than thirteen?

"I haven't ridden with anyone for . . . a long time."

He didn't count his *teammates*?

Was I seriously about to miss my chance to snowboard with D-Day?

No way.

"Come on," I urged him. "It'll be way more fun than hanging out by yourself."

"Hmm." He was still staring up the mountain.

"Just a few runs," I practically whined. "The sun's out, the powder's pretty fresh, and we're already geared up and ready to go."

He sighed, but half smiled. "Okay, let's do it."

"Yes!" I yelped, pumping a fist in the air.

He pushed off and started racing down the hill.

"You have to keep up, though," he shouted over his shoulder. "I'm not slowing down for you!"

"You won't have to," I whispered, going after him.

I hit a berm perfectly and flew into the air, hoping to gain some ground on the fast-disappearing D-Day, but he was already way ahead.

I'd always thought of him as a Slopestyle or Big Air star, since that's what he usually medalled in, but tricks weren't the only thing he'd mastered.

He competed in Boardercross too.

That was an awesome event to watch. Six pros, racing down a run like their lives depended on it. Skidding into turns, gapping the whoops and tucking so tight and low, it looked like they were sitting on their boards.

D-Day won a silver at his second-to-last Winter X Games.

He was *fast*.

But I was fast too.

Obviously, I wasn't a pro or anything, but that didn't mean I wasn't good.

I took a deep breath and bent my knees, making myself as compact as I could. The wind whipped against me and little flecks of snow stung my face.

Crazy or not, I was planning to do more than keep up.

The trees were nothing but a green blur, and the other boarders just slow-moving background for my awesome speed.

I caught another jump and flew into the air like a bird of prey. A wingless bird of prey, crunched into the smallest form possible for the sake of aerodynamics.

It was awesome!

That is, until I landed hard and had to make a super-tight turn.

I barely stayed upright.

Heart racing, I realized I might be going a little *too* fast. I speed-checked by turning the board to the side to slow it down a little.

Obviously, it was important for me to ride safe.

But I also needed to keep up with D-Day.

I could see his black shape ahead, getting smaller by the second. As much as I wanted to just tuck and go, I knew it was too dangerous for me to ride any faster.

The slower pace was more comfortable, but now my mind was racing.

What if I wasn't good enough to hang with him?

What if I got to the bottom of the run and he wasn't there?

What if he just took off? Ditched me?

What if I never had proof that I'd met him?

I hurried down the final stretch, moving as fast as I could while scanning the crowd near the lift for the guy in all black.

Had I blown my big chance to ride with a legend?

No!

Because there he was.

I buttered the end of the run, pulling out one of my smoother moves. (If my dad was there, I would have had to explain that "butter" meant a ground trick, but D-Day knew what I was doing.)

"Nosepress backside, huh?" he said, nodding when I came to a stop right in front of him. "Sweet."

"Thanks," I said, happy he liked it.

"You ride goofy?"

A couple of skiers turned to smirk, like D-Day was making fun of me, but any boarder knew that "goofy" just meant I rode with my right foot forward instead of "regular" with my left.

"Yeah," I said, releasing the board and moving into the lift line with him.

"Can you do a Backside Lipslide goofy?"

"Uh-huh." I nodded.

"Seriously?"

"Yeah. It took a *lot* of practice."

"No doubt," he said, chuckling. "Another run?"

"Definitely," I told him, grinning.

On the chairlift up, I couldn't stop wondering why he was hiding his identity. I mean, if I was a pro, I'd want *everybody* to know about it.

"My dad works for the mountain and he said Cody White snowboarded here," I said, hoping that might get him talking.

"Probably," he said, watching someone wipe out below us. "There are only so many mountains."

"It must be pretty cool to be a pro," I said, then waited for him to take the bait.

"Why's that?" he asked.

"Are you serious?" I gasped. "Getting paid to snowboard? Your picture in magazines? Free gear?"

D-Day shrugged. "I'll bet it's not as cool as it seems." He looked at me through my own goggle lenses as he changed the subject. "How long have you lived here?"

"A week," I told him.

That caught him off guard. "Really? But you said your dad worked for the mountain."

"He works for the Forest Service. We move around a lot."

"Must be nice," he said, nodding.

"Not really." When he looked confused, I explained, "Moving around means starting over at a new school every time."

"I guess that would be tough."

"It is," I said, with a sigh.

"How's it going in Timber so far?" he asked.

"Not very well," I said, swinging my feet.

"Oh."

I was glad he didn't ask me anything else for the rest of the ride up. When we got off the lift, we stood in front of the mountain's map and tried to choose a run.

"What about Graveyard?" he asked, pointing at a black line.

I checked the list and swallowed hard. "A triple black diamond?"

I'd never done one of those before.

"Yeah," he said, adjusting his goggles. "It'll get our juices flowing."

"Hmm." I might be able to take it at a normal speed, but trying to keep up with a pro on those kind of twists and turns wouldn't be easy.

"Come on," he said, elbowing me. "You're good enough."

What?

I wished I had a video camera or tape recorder with me so I could replay those words every day for the rest of my life. D-Day told me I was really good.

Unbelievable.

"Okay," I agreed, grinning. "Let's do this."

Within seconds, I was standing at the top of the run, knees shaking a little.

"Catch you at the bottom," he said, taking off.

Before I could chicken out and change my mind, I followed him.

Triple black diamond.

I leaned into the first turn, heart pounding.

Triple black diamond.

I hit a berm just right and landed smoothly.

It's just another run.

I bent my knees, bracing for another berm.

Triple black diamond run.

I built up speed and was too busy concentrating on making each turn to care about how far ahead of me D-Day was.

I didn't hear the other boarders or skiers. I didn't hear the birds in the trees or the people on the lifts. All I heard was the wind in my ears and the sound of my own ragged breathing.

It was awesome.

I came up on a tight corner and had to slow down when a skier in front of me bit it, hard. In a split second, he was face down in the snow, spread-eagled.

"You okay?" I called out to him.

"I'm good," he said, flashing a thumbs-up.

It was lucky I wasn't going top speed, because when I rounded the corner, I suddenly found myself at the top of the steepest slope I'd ever seen.

I turned hard and fast on my heelside edge, coming to a full stop with a spray of powder.

I looked straight down. It was like I was standing on top of a skyscraper.

Oh man.

My heart started hammering.

Triple black diamond.

I took a deep breath and searched for an all-black figure.

There he was! Already more than halfway down, rocketing toward the bottom like he had a jetpack strapped on his back.

I let out a low whistle.

This is serious.

I bent my knees a couple of times, keeping the blood flowing and trying to psych myself up.

All I had to do was make it to the bottom in one piece. It wasn't about speed, but control. D-Day was probably breaking a run record, but he was older than me with a lot more experience.

I wasn't a pro. I was a thirteen-year-old kid attempting my first ever *triple black diamond*.

"Go for it!" the guy who'd just wiped out shouted as he whipped past me and over the edge.

I watched him make it about twenty feet before losing his balance and landing on his back. It looked like it hurt, but he pulled himself back to his feet, adjusted his goggles and took off.

Two turns later, he was eating powder again. But he got up and got going.

I bent my knees a couple more times.

The worst thing that could happen is wiping out. That guy's done it three times in less than three minutes and it isn't stopping him.

I leaned forward and went for it.

I switched from heelside to toeside and back again, making long S-turns to keep my speed under control. It was pretty intense and I wobbled a couple of times before I wiped out.

I hit the ground face first and felt the snow slip down

the front of my jacket before melting against my neck. I lay there for a few seconds, then pushed myself back up on the board. I wiped off my goggles.

The worst thing that could happen already did, and I was just fine. A little embarrassed, but fine.

I shook the snow off and got moving.

Pacing myself, I worked my way through every obstacle, from tight turns to sudden drop-offs and big jumps to gnarly dips. I focused on keeping tight control of the board, no matter what.

And it was awesome!

When I reached the bottom of the run, D-Day was waiting for me.

"You good?" he asked.

"Yeah," I said, breathlessly.

"You look a little freaked out."

"That was my first triple black diamond."

"Ever?" he asked, sounding surprised.

I nodded. "Yeah."

"You should have said something. I could have—"

"It's cool," I told him. "I'm totally fine."

"You," he said, shaking his head and smiling, "are one tough little dude."

CHAPTER EIGHT

I had to keep an eye on the time, even though I hated to do it. Dad couldn't have made it any clearer that I had a six o'clock deadline for getting home. It was hard to believe how fast the minutes were whipping by, but the most awesome afternoon of my entire life was coming to an end.

When I checked my watch and saw that I had to go, I was seriously bummed out. We'd crammed in a bunch of runs and a ton of tricks, but three and a half hours had felt like only a couple of minutes.

"Ready?" D-Day asked, when I hesitated at the back of the lift line.

"Uh . . ."

For a split second, I considered one last run, but I knew that would be cutting it way too close. My parents would never let me snowboard "alone" again if

I blew off Dad's instructions the very first time I was allowed out solo.

"Salmon Derby?" D-Day suggested.

Come on.

That was the only one I hadn't been on yet.

A black diamond that was supposed to be all about big air.

Sighing, I shook my head. "I have to go home."

"Seriously?" he asked, surprised. "You can't do *one* more?"

I checked my watch again. "I'm going to be pushing it to get there on time already."

"Dude, it's finally dark. The lights are on, the runs are less busy. Come on."

Was Danny Day actually begging me to keep hanging out with him?

Yes, he was!

My brain took off at a sprint, imagining what it would be like if we became friends. Like, real friends, the kind where true identities were revealed.

What if we hung out for the entire Christmas break? Two weeks of non-stop action with D-Day? I'd pick up some awesome skills and it would be so cool to hear all about his life as a pro. What if he thought I had talent and he introduced me to his coach?

"Steven?"

My mental leash yanked my brain back to a much more serious question.

What if I walked in the door even one minute after Dad told me to? How terrible would my punishment be?

I gritted my teeth, wishing like crazy that I could say yes to just one more run.

But Mom would kill me.

"Uh . . . I have to be home by six. Dinner's at six-thirty," I explained.

"You have a reservation somewhere?"

"What?" My family only ate out for birthday dinners. "No, at home. Dinner's always at six-thirty."

He looked surprised. "Your whole family shows up?"

That had to be the weirdest question ever. "Yeah. I mean, Dad had to cover for someone at work, so he won't be there tonight. But he usually is."

"That's cool."

"It is?"

"Yeah." He wiped his nose with the back of a glove. "What are you having?"

"For dinner?" I asked, surprised that he cared. When he nodded, I shrugged and told him, "I don't know. Chicken or something, probably."

"I love chicken."

Weird. "Uh, same here, I guess." I took off my goggles and shoved them into my pack.

"Mashed potatoes or something with it?" he asked.

Were we still talking about dinner?

"I don't know about sides D—" I almost said D-Day

but caught myself again. "Derek. I'm not even sure it's chicken. It might be fish or pork, but no matter what it is, I have to be at the table and ready to dig in at six-thirty."

"Got it," he said, nodding.

"So, I better get going."

"Sure." He was quiet for a second, then said, "Hey, let me give these back to you. Thanks for the loan." He pulled off my old orange goggles and handed them to me.

"It's cool," I told him. "You can keep them." It was the least I could do after he'd given me the coolest afternoon ever.

"No, thanks," he said.

What was that supposed to mean? They were old, but they were still *cool.*

Weren't they?

I stared at the goggles he'd handed me. I still liked them. At least I thought I did.

"It was fun hanging out," he said. "You're pretty awesome."

"Thanks," I replied, doing my best not to scream.

D-Day thought I was awesome!

Wait, did he mean I was awesome, or my skills were? Or both?

"See you around," he said, heading back to the lift line.

"Hey!" I called after him, and when he turned I tossed him the goggles. "Just take them."

"Thanks."

"Sure." I watched him work his way toward the chair and wondered if I'd ever see him again. What were the chances of running into each other if we didn't plan it?

It doesn't matter, I reminded myself. I'd met a pro and even though I was totally awestruck to begin with, I'd held my own on the mountain.

I'd ridden with a pro.

Raced against a pro.

I'd spent hours boarding with D-Day.

D-Day!

My feet probably didn't touch the ground the whole way back to the house. I kept replaying bits of the afternoon over and over again in my head, like a DVD packed with highlights.

There was the time I actually *passed* him on Triple Tickle. Sure, I was only ahead for three seconds before he whipped by me and disappeared, but still. I'd passed him.

And when I watched him do a perfect Cross Rocket, I was the only person around who knew who he was. I was the world's only witness to total and absolute awesomeness!

I couldn't wait to tell my family about the amazing luck I'd had.

They weren't into snowboarding like I was, but I was sure they'd be almost as excited as I was.

But I was wrong.

★　★　★

I was out of breath by the time I got to the house, mostly because I'd run most of the way there.

Once I'd stomped the snow off my boots, I burst through the door and shouted, "You won't believe who I met on the mountain today."

"Who?" Thomas asked, from the TV room.

I hurried down the hallway, so I could see his face when I told him. "Guess."

My brother shrugged, his eyes still on his video game. "Um . . . The Rock?"

"What?"

"The Rock," he repeated, glancing at me, then back at the screen. "Dwayne Johnson."

I stared at him. "That's your guess?"

"You said I won't believe who you met."

"I know, but—"

"*The Rock* is someone I wouldn't believe you met."

"Can you be serious?"

He shot me a dirty look. "I *am* being serious."

I took a deep breath, concentrating on the awesome news instead of why my brother had to ruin it. "Okay, let's try again. This is someone I ran into while *snowboarding*, Thomas."

He turned back to his game. "The Rock doesn't snowboard?"

"I have no idea. Look, it wasn't him, okay? Can you just pick someone else?"

"But that was my best guess."

"Come on, Thomas."

He shook his head. "I don't like this game."

"What game?" Mom asked, stopping in the doorway with a laundry basket balanced against her hip.

I had a second chance to get the excitement rolling! "Guess who I met on the mountain today?"

"Someone you *won't believe*," Thomas added.

Mom thought for a few seconds before guessing, "Katy Perry?"

"The singer?" I asked, totally confused.

Mom nodded. "Or maybe Taylor Swift?"

"What?" My head was spinning. "Why would either of them be *here*? Why would The Rock be here?"

"That was my guess," Thomas explained.

"So, what's yours, Mom?"

Thomas turned to me, rolling his eyes. "Can't you just tell us who it was?"

"Guess," I demanded, wanting to recapture the excitement I'd been feeling.

"We already did," he said, folding his arms across his chest.

"Is it Tom Cruise? Is he filming a movie?" Mom asked, using her free hand to fix her hair, like he was going to show up on our doorstep at any second.

"No. No one's filming a movie."

"Then how did The Rock become part of this conversation?"

"Steven told me to guess who I wouldn't believe he'd run into on the mountain and The Rock was my guess," Thomas explained.

"What?" Mom asked.

"It doesn't matter," I told her.

They were going to drive me nuts!

Especially when Thomas started killing martians and Mom started to walk toward the kitchen.

I was losing my audience!

"Look, if you're not going to guess, I'll just tell you," I threatened.

"Okay," Thomas said.

"*Come on.* You're really not going to guess?" I begged.

"I've got to check on the roast, honey," Mom said over her shoulder.

"Okay, okay!" I said, giving up. "I'll tell you."

They looked at each other and shrugged.

"So?" Thomas said. "Who was it?"

I grinned. "You're seriously not going to believe this."

"So we hear," Mom said, glancing toward the kitchen.

"This was like the shock of a lifetime," I reminded them. "Unbelievable."

"Message received," Thomas said, nodding.

"Are you ready?" I asked.

"Steven," Mom warned, and I knew I'd run out of time.

I took a deep breath.

"D-Day!" I shouted.

Mom and Thomas looked at each other, then at me. At the exact same time, they both asked, "*Who?*"

"D-Day," I repeated. "Danny Day. Snowboarding legend?"

Thomas frowned. "Maybe?"

"Maybe what?"

"You just asked if he's a snowboarding legend."

"No, I *told* you he is."

Thomas shook his head. "It sounded like a question."

"Well, it wasn't," I snapped.

"I thought you liked Cody White."

"I *do* like . . . will you just listen?" I snapped.

"Calm down, Steven," Mom said.

But I couldn't calm down. They were destroying the biggest and best moment of my life like it was nothing! "You guys don't get it. I'm talking about the one and only D-Day."

"The snowboarder," Mom said, with a nod. "Pretty exciting."

I could tell she still had no idea who I was talking about. Maybe she needed to hear the whole story to get the full impact.

I told her and Thomas about the mysterious guy in black I'd seen all over the mountain and how I'd literally run into him. I explained that he was using another name, and Thomas cut me off.

"Hold on, Steven." He glanced at Mom, then back at me. "He told you his name was *Derek*?"

"Yeah. I figure he's keeping a low profile—"

He held up a hand to stop me. "Or he's not D-Day."

"But he *is*, Thomas." I knew exactly who I'd spent my afternoon with. My little brother had no idea what he was talking about. "Wait here," I told him, and started to run upstairs.

"The roast is calling me," Mom said, heading down the hallway.

"Just give me a second, okay? I'll meet you in the kitchen."

"Whatever," I heard Thomas snort.

I ran into my room and straight to the stack of magazines next to my bed. I flipped past the first few before I found what I was looking for.

"Ha!" I said, lifting a copy of *Boarder* magazine and admiring the shot of D-Day on the cover.

I ran downstairs, waving the magazine in the air.

"See?" I shouted, pointing at the photo.

"What?" Thomas asked, wrinkling his nose.

"That's him," I said, tapping the cover with my finger. "D-Day."

"Cool," he said, with a nod.

"I'm serious. This is D-Day. Right here."

"Fine." Thomas stared at me. "I didn't say he didn't *exist*, Steven."

"Well good, because he does."

"Yeah." He paused and pointed at the cover. "But that doesn't mean *he's* Derek."

"He *isn't* Derek," I practically choked.

"I mean the Derek you hung out with today."

"I swear to you that *this*," I stabbed the magazine with my fingertip, "is the guy I spent the afternoon with." I took a ragged breath. "*D-Day.*"

"The magazine doesn't prove anything, Steven," Thomas told me, as he lifted a drink box to his mouth. He grabbed a magazine from the top of Mom's stack and pointed at the cover photo. "I could tell you I ran into this guy on Pine Road today and—"

"He's dead," I said, recognizing the actor, who'd been killed in a car crash.

"Okay, that was a bad example. If I saw—"

"Why can't you just let me have this?" I asked.

Thomas looked puzzled. "Have what?"

"This one cool thing that happened to me. This one cool day out of a crummy week."

"I didn't mean—"

"Forget it," I said, heading for the stairs.

"Steven!" my little brother called after me.

"I said forget it!" I snapped over my shoulder.

As soon as I reached my room, I slammed the door and rested the back of my head against it.

I would not let them destroy the most amazing thing that had ever happened to me.

No way.

After I'd calmed down, I flopped on my bed with the magazine I'd shown Thomas. There D-Day was, right in front of me. It didn't seem possible that I'd just spent a chunk of the day with him.

But I had.

If only I'd taken a picture. If only he'd admitted who he was.

I opened the magazine to the D-Day article. Of course, I'd read it before, but I hadn't known him back then. I read through it again, absorbing every word and hearing every quote in D-Day's voice in my head.

I never would have dreamed I'd meet a real live pro, unless I became one myself.

For a second or two, I wondered what he meant when he said being a pro probably wasn't as cool as it seemed.

I couldn't think of a single thing about it that *wouldn't* be cool.

I closed my eyes and imagined my own face on the cover of that magazine. The kids at Evergreen would feel pretty bad when I became a millionaire superstar.

And they wouldn't be the only ones. I thought back to all of the towns I'd lived in and wondered how many people would be amazed by what I'd become and regret never giving me a chance.

Too bad for them.

CHAPTER NINE

Since I'd made it home on time, I asked if I could go snowboarding alone again the next day. It was partly because I didn't want to hang out with Thomas, but mostly because I hoped there was some way I could track D-Day down.

I knew the chances of that happening were pretty slim, but I couldn't help it.

"I'm thirteen," I reminded my parents, when I made the request. "A teenager." I paused. "A *responsible* teenager."

"I don't know," Mom said, folding her arms.

"I've never given you guys any reason to think I'll get in trouble."

"True," Dad agreed.

"Everything was fine today," I added. "I got home on time, no problem."

"Also true," Dad said, which gave me the feeling he was rooting for me.

"Don't you think I've earned the chance to do it again?" I asked, hopefully.

Mom and Dad gave each other a long look before Mom finally said that it would be okay, if I folded the laundry that night. That was fine with me. As far as punishments went, mine was turning out to be gravy.

"You'll take Dad's phone with you on the mountain," Mom said.

It was about a hundred years old, but I didn't care. "Sure," I told her.

In the morning, I shoved some extra granola bars and a couple of bottles of water into my pack, just in case I ran into a certain legend. D-Day didn't seem to carry much with him, so I wanted to have enough for both of us if I was lucky enough to hang with him again.

"You'll be home by six," Dad said.

I nodded. "Definitely."

"Do you *have to* go on your own?" Mom asked, then bit her lip. "There aren't any friends from school you could invite?"

I heard Thomas choke on a laugh from his spot in front of the TV.

"I don't have any *friends*, Mom." I'd told her the

same thing about every school in every town we'd ever lived in.

She looked at Dad, who nodded and handed me his phone. "You're a responsible kid, Steven. Let's keep it that way, okay?"

"I will," I promised.

I ran upstairs to get changed and grabbed a couple of magazines with D-Day on their covers while I was at it. I found a felt pen and put all of it into my pack, just in case.

"What about breakfast?" Mom asked, when I headed straight for the front door. "You're not leaving this house on an empty stomach."

Little did she know, it wasn't empty at all. It was jam-packed with excitement.

To make her happy, I peeled a banana and wolfed it down in two bites.

"That's not—"

"Granola bars in my bag," I told her, through a mouthful of mush.

"Call me at noon, so I know you're okay."

"I'll be fine, Mom."

"News I'll be delighted to hear when you call me *at noon*," she said, firmly.

"Fine," I said, hurrying toward the door.

"Later," Thomas called, from his spot in the living room.

"Yup," I told him, still annoyed.

117

As soon as I was outside, I started walking fast, then jogging, until I was practically running full-speed toward the lifts.

In between each gasping breath, I searched for a figure in black, hoping like crazy that I'd see him.

"On your way to a liars' convention?" a voice called from across the street.

My stomach lurched as I turned to see Nolan and Tyler cracking up.

"He's the guest speaker!" Tyler said, barely getting the words out.

"Why aren't you carpooling with Cody White?" Nolan asked.

I did my best to ignore them, even when a snowball nailed me in the back of the head. They laughed so hard and for so long, I could hear them when I was a block away.

No one was going to forget my White Lie over the break. That was for sure.

I tried to push the whole mess out of my head as I arrived at the lift line. I had two weeks of freedom before I had to go back to school, so I might as well enjoy it. And if I could enjoy it with a legend, that was even better.

I rode the lift up by myself, my eyes glued to the runs below me, looking for D-Day. But I didn't see him anywhere.

When I got off the lift, I decided my best bet was

a double black diamond, and since he'd mentioned Salmon Derby when I had to leave the day before, I started there.

After the first couple of jumps, I realized a warm-up run or two might have been a good idea. It took all of my concentration to make the gnarly turns, so I couldn't keep my eyes peeled for him at the same time. Not unless I wanted to seriously crash, anyway.

I rode the lift up again, but luck wasn't with me. I didn't see an all-black figure anywhere.

But he saw me.

"Steven!" he called from the lift line before my fifth run.

"Hey!" I waved, grinning like a maniac, and joined him in line.

"I should have grabbed your cell number yesterday," he said, pulling out a phone.

"Oh, I don't have a phone," I admitted, totally embarrassed as I gave him our new home number. "My parents said I could get one next year."

"How old are you?" he asked.

"Thirteen."

"No way," he said. "You seem older."

"I do?" I asked, stunned.

"Yeah. You're a way better boarder than most thirteen-year-olds."

D-Day said I, Steven White, was *a way better boarder* than most thirteen-year-olds. I thought my head was going to explode, but I managed to stay calm. Kind of.

I don't know whether it was because of the rotten week I'd had at school or the fact that I was riding with D-Day, but I had more fun than ever before on my board.

The sun was shining, the powder was fresh, and every trick I pulled was close to perfect.

When we sat at a picnic table to take a break around lunchtime, D-Day was smiling as much as I was.

"I haven't done this for a long time."

"Done what?" I asked.

"Ridden with someone, just for fun."

I waited for him to tell me who he really was, but he got sidetracked by the granola bars, shoving a second one into his mouth. Then he opened his pack. "I have some drinks here, if you want one."

"Power Blitz," I said, reaching for a can.

He handed both to me. "I hate the stuff."

"Really?" I asked. He was sponsored by Power Blitz.

"Yeah. I've got cases and just want to get rid of it."

"Why do you have cases if you don't like it?"

I waited for his answer, knowing it was the perfect time for him to tell me he was a pro and he had a deal with the company.

"Oh . . . uh, my mom won a contest."

My heart sunk. Why couldn't he just tell me the truth?

★　★　★

For the next couple of days we got into a routine, starting with meeting in front of my house at eight every morning.

I never brought him inside, because I couldn't trust my family not to blurt out his real name. My parents were just happy I was having fun, so Mom baked awesome treats for me to take each day and limited her contact to a wave from the window.

So, I brought the lunches and D-Day brought the skills.

It was *awesome*.

We'd ride our boards all day, whipping past skiers and catching air wherever we could. We laughed, joked and had tons of fun together. I realized that he wasn't going to tell me who he was and I kind of got over it. After all, I was hanging out with him, whether he knew I knew it or not.

When we were done for the day, he'd give me a ride home in his black Jeep, then take off. He never invited me to his place but I knew it was on Pine. I got Mom to drive me down there once and figured he was at the one with the big gate.

We never talked about *why* we never visited each other's places. Of course, I knew I didn't want him to see his posters on my walls, but it wasn't like he had pictures of me on *his*. Maybe he was embarrassed that his house was bigger and more awesome than mine.

Maybe he didn't want me to meet his parents. Maybe he just wanted a little privacy. Whatever the reason was, it didn't really matter. I only needed to see him on the slopes.

Dad and I went shopping on Wednesday, so I could help him find a present for Mom. As usual, she'd refused to make a wish list like the rest of us, because she wanted to be surprised.

And she definitely would have been surprised if I let Dad buy her a blender.

"No one wants a blender, Dad."

"But she—"

"*No one*," I repeated, firmly. "Not as a Christmas present." I led the way toward the robes and slippers. "She's always saying the kitchen's too cold in the morning and her stuff is pretty old."

"You're right." Dad smiled. "That's perfect!"

As soon as we'd picked a set in light blue, we headed up to the counter to pay. And as soon as we got to the back of the line, I recognized two girls in front of us from school.

I didn't know their names, but they were both in my Math class. It didn't take long for them to notice me, and then the giggling and whispering began.

Dad raised an eyebrow at me.

I shrugged back.

"Hi, Steven," the one with the curly hair said, then started giggling again.

"Hi," I answered, hoping the conversation would end there.

It didn't.

"Christmas shopping?" the other one asked.

"Uh-huh," I said, nodding.

"Nice," Curly said, looking at the robe.

"It's for my mom," I told them.

"Cool," the other one said, then stared at Dad.

"Hi," he said, smiling. "I'm—"

"Cody White?" Curly said, then both girls snorted with laughter.

Dad looked confused. "John White, actually."

They laughed even louder.

"My dad," I said, hoping that would quiet them down.

Luckily, the cashier was ready for them in a couple of minutes and they lost interest in us.

"Cody White? What was that all about?" Dad asked, when we stepped up to the register.

"Nothing."

And I wished it was true.

"Girls from school?" he asked, as he handed the cashier his credit card.

"Yeah, but I don't really know them."

"Cody White," he murmured. "That was strange."

"I need to find something for Thomas," I told him, trying to change the subject.

"What are you looking for?"

"I don't know. Something to do with video games, I guess."

"I think there's a store upstairs," he said, leading the way.

From the escalator, I saw a sporting-goods store with ski gear and snowboarding stuff in the front window. If I wasn't shopping for Thomas, I would have loved to look around.

"I saw your list," Dad said, watching me. "I thought you'd want all kinds of new gear."

I did. I wanted the Green Beast, but didn't want to ask for it. Money was tight at our house and it wasn't exactly cheap. "Some gloves would be cool," I told him, wishing I could say a lot more.

"Gloves," he repeated. "Gotcha."

As I watched the sporting-goods store disappear from view, I thought it might be cool to get D-Day something for Christmas. After all, he was the only friend I had.

Then again, he probably had everything he could ever want. And if he didn't, he could just go out and buy it.

So why didn't he pick up some new Oakley goggles? He'd been wearing mine almost every day. Maybe he only liked that style, which no one sold anymore.

"Hey, Steven," a voice called from the top of the escalator.

I looked up to see Glitter Morgan smiling at me.

"Hey," I said.

"Are you Christmas shopping?"

"Yeah." Wasn't every single person in the mall doing the same thing?

Before she could make a Cody White comment like the other girls had, I hurried Dad toward the big sign for the gaming store.

"She seemed nice," Dad said.

"I think Thomas might want a new headset," I told him. "Let's see if any of them are on sale."

When we got home with a couple of shopping bags each and an empty wallet for me, I headed straight for the fridge. But I barely had the door open and was pushing past the milk to get to some orange juice when I heard Mom's voice.

"Your friend is upstairs," she said.

"What?" I asked, confused.

"Derek," she said, like it was nothing. Like it wasn't enough to totally freak me out. "He's in your room."

I closed my eyes for a second, and all I could see was the D-Day poster that hung right over my desk.

"Danny?" I whispered.

"Whatever his name is today," Mom said, laughing.

"No!" I gasped.

"What's wrong?"

"The posters, the magazines. Everything!"

She stared at me. "I have no idea what you're talking about."

"He's in my room."

She nodded. "I told him he could wait for you there, if he felt like it."

"Mom, his face is all over the . . ." I couldn't even finish the sentence.

"What on earth is the problem, Steven?"

"He's going to know that I *know!*"

Mom just stared at me, like I'd lost my mind.

And maybe I had.

She shook her head. "What do you know?"

"That he's D-Day," I whispered.

"D-Day?" she asked, like she'd never heard the name before.

I groaned. I guess I didn't need to worry about her spilling the beans if she didn't even have them.

"I *told* you about this. He's only calling himself Derek. He's really Danny. Danny Day. D-Day. Oh, never mind," I sighed, and ran for the stairs.

"Do you want some cookies to take up?" Mom called after me.

Did she really think *cookies* would fix this?

"No thanks," I called over my shoulder as I took the stairs two at a time.

When I got to the landing, I froze.

What the heck was I going to say?

I couldn't pretend I didn't recognize him when he was standing next to a poster of *his own face*.

I took a couple of deep breaths as I tried to think of something, *anything,* to say. I closed my eyes, but everything was blank, like a big white snowdrift.

As tempted as I was to just stand there forever, I knew I had to open the door.

And I did.

There was no way he didn't hear the squeaking door hinge, but D-Day didn't move a muscle. He just stood with his back to me, staring at my wall of posters.

I cleared my throat, feeling nervous.

He turned around, and I couldn't tell what the expression on his face meant. He didn't look sad or angry, but blank, like my snowdrift.

"So," I began, but had no idea where to go from there.

"So," he repeated, quietly.

Then the room was totally silent. D-Day turned back to the wall of posters. He probably knew most or even all of the guys on my wall. He'd beaten some and lost to others.

I waited for something to happen, but nothing did.

The picture of D-Day and Jimmy Wagner battling for first place seemed to have his full attention. Did he remember how close that finish was?

Who was I kidding?

Of course he remembered. I'd admired the posters

every day for as long as I could remember, but he'd actually been there. He'd *lived* the moments I could only dream about.

I was about to tell him how awesome his *Big Air* cover was when he turned around to face me.

"How long have you known?" he asked.

I thought about playing dumb and asking what he was talking about, but it seemed kind of pointless.

"Since I met you."

"Huh," he said, shaking his head. "Why didn't you say anything?"

I shrugged. "You told me your name was Derek."

"True," he said, sitting on the edge of my bed.

I sat in my desk chair and swivelled back and forth a couple of times, getting up the nerve to be nosy.

"So, why did you say you were someone else?" I asked.

He laughed, but only for a second. "I don't know. I was tired of being me, I guess."

"Are you kidding?" I gasped, sure that my eyes were bugging out of my head. "Everyone wants to be you!"

"Everyone?" he asked, raising one eyebrow.

I thought about it for a second before answering, "Well, probably not movie stars and stuff, but regular people do. People like me. I mean, *I* do."

He shook his head. "You want to be me?"

"Well . . . yeah."

"You're nuts."

"I'm nuts? You're a totally famous pro snowboarder.

You've won championships, D-Day!" I gulped. "Oh, is it okay if I call you that?"

"Can you just call me Danny?"

I shrugged. "I guess. So, you've won championships, you're on magazine covers. You have a couple of DVDs out—"

"Not as good as Cody White's *Whiteout*, I hear," he interrupted.

I nearly choked. "Sorry about that."

He gave me half a smile. "It's okay, Steven."

"You've got this awesome life, and I guess I don't understand why you don't want to be *you*."

"I'm guessing you've heard of the X Games."

"Sure." I nodded.

"So, I'm sure you know what happened the last time I competed."

"You lost," I practically whispered, picturing that horrible crash.

"Lost? I totally blew it. I was trying to pull a—"

"Locust 1080."

"You've seen it," he said, glumly.

"Yeah." About a hundred times.

"And you're still asking why I'd rather not be me?"

I shrugged. "It was one mistake." I saw the look on his face and hurried to say, "I know it was a big one—"

"Huge."

"Okay, a huge one, but that doesn't mean you have to go into hiding and—"

129

"I'm not in *hiding*. I'm just . . . laying low."

I frowned. "You're using a fake name. In the middle of nowhere. That's hiding."

"Can you blame me?"

I thought back to the footage and had to say "No."

We were both quiet for a few minutes, and when it started to get awkward, Danny lifted one of the magazines from my stack. Lee Jarvis was on the cover.

"What's he like?" I asked.

"Lee?"

"Yeah."

"Kind of a jerk," he said. "Good snowboarder, lame person."

"He always seems so cool in the interviews," I said, but Danny didn't respond.

Instead, he flipped through the pages of the magazine.

"So, do you guys hang out?" I asked.

"Me and Lee?"

"No, I mean all the pros."

He shrugged. "When we're at competitions, a little. I've gone on a couple of European trips with Matty Doakes, to film videos and—"

"*Arctic Blast*, one and two," I said.

"Uh, yeah."

"I have both," I told him, "in my DVD library."

"Cool," he said, nodding.

"So, you're friends with the other guys?"

"Not all of them, but some."

Some was cool enough for me.

The room was quiet as he flipped through pages and I realized that he was the only person I knew who could get me out of my mess at school.

I took a moment to try to figure out the best way to make my request and decided being honest would be a nice change of pace.

I cleared my throat. "Can I ask you a favour?"

He shrugged. "I guess so."

"Okay, there's this *situation* at school."

He looked up from the pages of *Boarder*. "Situation?"

"Yeah. You know how I told you I'm new in town?"

"Sure."

"Well, I've been new in a lot of towns, and it's really hard. Know what I mean?"

He nodded. "Making new friends, finding your way around and all that."

"Exactly," I said, smiling. "So, I decided to try something different this time. I decided to stand out as something other than the new kid." I took a deep breath. "So I kind of told the other kids I'm Cody White's cousin."

He snorted with laughter. "What? *Why?*"

"I thought being a celebrity could help me out."

"But you're not the celebrity. Cody is."

"Right, but I'm *part* celebrity because I'm related to him."

"Except that you're not."

I felt my face turn red. "Exactly."

There was a long silence before Danny asked, "What's the favour, Steven?"

I started to feel excited. "If you could come to Evergreen with me on the first day back, or meet me there or whatever and—"

"What?"

"If you could come with me to school and tell the kids that Cody White really *is* my cousin—"

He shook his head. "That wouldn't solve your problem."

"It totally would. They think I'm a liar."

"Only because you *lied*, Steven."

"Yeah, but if *you* said it was the truth—"

"I'd be a liar too." He sighed. "I'm not interested."

"*Danny.*"

The plan was brilliant.

I was brilliant.

Why couldn't he just play along?

"What's one tiny lie? You'll never see those kids again, anyway."

Danny stared at me like I was from another planet. "What makes you so sure they'd believe me?"

"Because you *know* Cody White. I mean, you're D-Day."

"I'm *Danny.*" He growled. "Have you been listening to me at all?"

"What? Of course!"

"Okay, because a couple of minutes ago I told you I wanted a break from being D-Day."

I nodded. "I know."

"I wanted to lay low and be someone else for a while."

"Yeah."

"And now you want to parade me around your school?"

What?

"Hold on. I never said *parade*."

He crossed his arms. "What would you call it?"

I shrugged. "Vouching for me?"

"Lying for you."

"No! Not *for* me. More . . . *with* me."

He shook his head. "Not gonna happen."

I couldn't believe what I was hearing! "But it would only take a few minutes and—"

"The answer's no, Steven. Please don't ask me again."

CHAPTER TEN

Mom invited Danny to stay for dinner and I didn't think there was a chance he'd want to hang out with my family, but I was wrong. Way wrong.

Not only did he want to stay, he was actually *excited* about meat loaf.

No joke. Meat loaf.

"I haven't had a home-cooked meal in forever," he said, helping himself to some mashed potatoes, then drowning them with gravy.

Mom turned toward him, surprised. "Your parents don't cook?"

He shook his head. "They do, but they're in Colorado."

Mom glanced at Dad, then back at Danny. "Who's looking after you?"

Danny shrugged. "I'm sixteen."

Mom put her fork down, too disturbed to eat. "That's what I mean. Who is looking after you?"

He looked right into her eyes. "I am."

Mom raised one eyebrow at Dad, like she was tagging him in.

"Uh, where are you staying?" Dad asked.

"My old coach's cabin. I'm totally fine there. The freezer's stocked and—"

"Freezer?" Mom interrupted.

"Yeah," he said, smiling. "I've got pizza, chicken strips—"

"That sounds awesome," Thomas said.

"No, it doesn't," Mom said, shaking her head.

For the first time since I'd slammed the door on him, I was with Thomas. Pizza and chicken strips? Bring it on!

"Wait," Mom said. "You said you're staying *at* your old coach's cabin, not *with* him."

"I think what we're curious about," Dad interrupted, "is—"

Mom cut him off there. "Who else is there with you?"

Uh-oh. She was in total mom mode.

I needed to jump in and help him out (even though he wasn't doing the same for me with the kids at school).

"Can you pass the peas?" I asked Thomas, who handed them to me. I tried to bang the spoon around in the bowl to make some distracting noise, but that wasn't enough.

"Is there an adult with you?" Mom asked Danny.

"No, it's just me."

"Sweet!" Thomas said, like *he* could actually take care of himself if he had the chance.

"Mom still cuts the crusts off your sandwiches," I reminded him, and he gave me a dirty look.

Our fight wasn't over yet.

Mom glanced at Dad, then said, "A sixteen-year-old, eating frozen pizza—"

"I'm sure he heats it up first," I said, leaping to Danny's defense.

Mom held up a hand to stop me. "Eating frozen pizza in an abandoned cabin."

"It's not abandoned," Danny explained, "it's just—"

"Why are you there alone?" Dad asked.

Danny shrugged. "I needed some time to myself. I just needed to lay low for a little while."

"Needed to *lay low*?" Mom repeated. She gave him a suspicious look, like he was a criminal or something.

"It's because of the X Games," I explained, hoping to take the heat off him.

Danny gave me a look. "I don't really want to talk about—"

"What happened?" Thomas asked.

"Never mind," I muttered, wishing I'd kept my big mouth shut.

Danny had been touchy since I told him about my master plan, and suddenly I had no idea what would annoy him from one minute to the next.

"It's a secret?" Thomas asked.

"Let it go," I snapped.

"I'm not talking to you, Steven," my little brother replied.

"*Mom*," I said, giving her a pleading look she seemed to understand.

"Thomas, mind your own—"

"I crashed," Danny interrupted. "I tried to pull a big trick and I blew it. I ruined everything for me, my sponsors and my family."

Thomas stared at him. "This is about one little crash?"

"It wasn't little," I said, then saw Danny's frown. "I mean, it was kind of a big deal."

"And you're ashamed," Thomas said.

"Well, embarrassed," Danny corrected.

Thomas shrugged. "Same thing."

"Thomas, just leave it alone," I snapped, and caught a grateful look from Danny.

I felt my shoulders relax. I was back on his good side.

"What about Christmas?" Mom suddenly asked.

Danny looked confused. "What about it?"

"What are you doing for Christmas dinner?"

"I think my folks are going to try to make it out here."

Mom looked at Dad again. "He *thinks* they're *trying* to make it out here."

"Yeah," Danny said. "It depends on how bad the snow is. They've been cancelling flights and stuff."

"That's it," Mom said. "You're staying with us."

"What?" I practically choked. I was totally embarrassed that Mom was treating him like some kind of charity case. Sure, he was sixteen years old, but the guy was *rich*. Even if he didn't have the use of the cabin, he could stay at whatever fancy hotel he wanted.

And we didn't even have a guest room, anyway! Did she really think a pro snowboarder would want to share a room with me?

Hold on.

Why was I questioning that plan?

Hanging with Danny twenty-four-seven would be totally sweet!

And if kids from school saw us together? Even better!

"I'm okay where I am. Thank you for the invitation, though," he said.

"But—" Mom began.

I was pretty disappointed when he added, "I'm totally fine, Mrs. White. I really do need some time alone."

"But on *Christmas*? You've got to at least come for dinner. Turkey, stuffing, blackberry pie . . ."

There was no way *D-Day* would spend Christmas at my dinner table. He had way better places to—

"That would be awesome," he said, grinning.

"Seriously?" I gasped.

Was there any better Christmas present than Danny Day as a guest?

What if he brought presents for us? A new board was a big expense for my family, but it would be nothing for him!

I started grinning too.

"What can I bring?" he asked.

I was ready to write him a list, until Mom said, "Nothing. No food, no gifts. Absolutely nothing."

What?

Was she crazy?

I didn't have time to ask, because Danny had tasted his first bite of meat loaf and couldn't stop telling her how delicious it was.

For the rest of the meal, I watched my family treat the legendary D-Day like . . . a regular person. It was totally weird, but kind of cool at the same time.

After dinner, Danny helped clear the table and played some vampire video game with Thomas before we headed back up to my room.

Seeing him surrounded by posters of himself and people he actually knew was still weird for me, but he seemed comfortable.

"Your family is really nice," he said.

"I guess," I said, with a shrug.

"I miss that. Dinner around the table and all that stuff."

"Really?"

139

"Yeah. It might seem boring now, but if you didn't have it for months at a time, you'd miss it too."

I doubted that.

"You really miss being boring?" I asked.

"Not boring. *Normal.*"

"Same thing," I told him.

"It isn't the same at all."

"All I know is, I'd trade places with you in two seconds, flat."

We made plans to hang out on the mountain together the next day. I brought the sandwiches and we hit the runs hard.

The coolest thing about hanging with a pro was all of the little tricks and tips he shared with me, like standing on the board on the carpet at home. It was amazing how much better my balance was after practising in my bedroom. He also told me to get my stance width adjusted on my board, since I was both taller and heavier than I'd been when I got it.

My snowboarding skills were better than ever, but what I *really* needed help with was my social situation.

Danny had refused to back up my Cody White story at school, but what if we just happened to run into some of the kids while we were on the mountain? If he could take care of it right then and there, he probably would. Wouldn't he?

I kept my eyes peeled for someone from school, and I mean *anyone*, but I didn't recognize a single face. After all the times I'd run into kids who gave me dirty looks or ignored me, I couldn't believe it. I watched the lift lines and the chairs themselves, the tables at the Summit café and even the bunny hill, but for once I didn't see a soul I knew.

"So, what's the best part of being a pro?" I asked, on the lift that afternoon.

"I don't know," he said, shrugging.

I tried another angle. "Of the guys on your team, who's your favourite?"

"Like I told you before, we don't really hang out that much."

I stared at him. "But you're teammates."

"Yeah, teammates competing against each other in some events."

I hadn't thought about that. When Team Burton snagged first and second place, one of the guys had beaten the other.

"When you were at the last Winter X Games—"

"I don't want to talk about that."

"But the Locust 1080 was—"

"I just said I don't want to talk about it," he snapped.

The last thing I wanted to do was tick him off, so I let it go.

We raced down the next run and it was hard to keep up with him, but I managed.

"Wow," I said, slightly out of breath when we walked toward the lift line. "You were *hauling*."

He nodded but didn't say anything. And that's when I spotted none other than Nolan and Tyler.

The worst jerks of all, just ten feet ahead of us, at the back of the lift line.

It was perfect!

I led the way over to them, my heart pounding in my chest. This was going to be *awesome*. I pulled off my goggles as Danny moved into the spot next to me.

"Hey," I said, poking Nolan in the back.

He spun around, smiling until he saw my face and groaned. "Oh, it's you."

"Yeah," I said. "It's me." I couldn't help grinning when I pointed to my right. "Me and D-Day."

I felt him stiffen next to me, but ignored it. We'd make this quick and easy, like tearing off a Band-Aid. All of my problems would be solved in two seconds, flat.

Nolan glanced at the pro, then back at Tyler. They both snorted.

"What?" I demanded.

"Give it up, man," Tyler said.

"Give what up . . . No, seriously. This is D-Day." I turned to look at my friend, who was wearing a pair of mirrored red goggles.

I lifted a hand to my own eyes and made a flicking gesture, so he'd take them off.

But D-Day didn't move.

"Your goggles," I whispered, flicking my hand again. This time, the effort was a little more frantic.

He just stood there.

"Lame," Nolan said, laughing.

"*So* lame," Tyler echoed.

"Take off your goggles," I hissed at D-Day. When he still didn't move or speak, I quietly begged, "Please."

Nolan shook his head. "You're like the most desperate, weird kid I've ever met."

"Yeah," Tyler snorted. "Get a life."

"Your *own* life," Nolan added.

I couldn't make a sound. My mouth was dry and my cheeks were red hot with embarrassment. I watched them get on the next chair, and when I turned around to chew D-Day out, he was gone.

"You going up?" the liftie asked, as the next chair came at me.

"Uh, no," I told her, spotting the all-black boarder walking away.

I raced through the crowd, apologizing to people as I banged into them, and when I caught up to my "friend," I was sweaty, out of breath and ticked off.

"What was that about?" I asked, jumping in front of him.

"You tell me."

"Come on, man. All you had to do was show your face."

143

He lifted his goggles and glared at me. "All you had to do was leave me out of it."

"Are you being serious?"

"Absolutely. I told you I'm laying low right now."

"I know, but you couldn't have just taken them off for, like, two seconds?" I snapped.

"No."

"But that would have fixed everything."

"Fixed everything?" He stared at me. "No, it wouldn't."

"Of *course* it would. They could have seen me hanging out with you." I was so frustrated, I could barely talk. "You wouldn't have even had to tell them I was Cody's cousin."

"Wow. Thanks, Steven."

"No. I mean, it would have been enough that I *know* you. D-Day."

"It's *Danny*, and who cares who you know?"

"Seriously?" I asked.

"Why can't you just be . . . you?"

"You're kidding, right?"

"Why do you care so much about what those two think, anyway?"

"It's not just them. It's . . . everybody. They all hate me."

"You really turned an *entire* school against you?"

I thought about Ethan and Glitter Morgan.

"Most of them, anyway."

"And you did it all in a single week?"

I nodded. "Well, five days."

"Because you lied," he said, and when I didn't respond, he asked, "So why do you want to keep *lying?*"

I felt my shoulders slump.

Danny didn't understand. And how could he? The guy was a pro snowboarder. He was famous. He had everything.

He didn't have to worry about making friends.

I groaned. "I just don't get why you couldn't take off the goggles."

"And I don't get why you'd ask me to, Steven. I told you I just wanted to be someone else for a while."

"I know, but—"

"You *don't* know," he said, shaking his head. "And until you figure it out, I don't really want to hang with you."

"What?"

"You heard me," he said, turning and walking away.

CHAPTER ELEVEN

The next couple of days were the worst.

I was lonely and bored out of my mind. Obviously, I'd had an awesome time boarding with Danny, but I hadn't realized exactly *how* awesome it was, or just how lonely I'd been before he came along.

And now I was even lonelier.

There was only so much time I could spend flipping through magazines I'd already read a hundred times, and even my favourite trick DVDs weren't doing anything for me.

But the worst part of all was that I was finally allowed to hit the mountain solo, and I didn't feel like it.

I'm not sure if I was more worried about running into Danny or the kids from school, but for the first time in as long as I could remember, I wanted to do anything *but* snowboard.

"Need help?" I asked Mom, who was busy on the laptop at the kitchen table.

"With bills?" she asked, winking at me. "Do you have a secret stash of cash I don't know about?"

"No." I wished! If I had enough money, maybe I could *buy* some friends. But I was broke.

"Is something wrong?"

I shook my head. "No."

She gave me a long look. "I'll take your word for it, but you look grim."

"I'm not," I practically growled.

"Message received, Steven," she said, a warning in her voice. "Watch your tone."

"Sorry."

Her sigh sounded pretty frustrated. "If you need something to do, how about setting the table?"

"Okay," I told her, and pulled four checkered place-mats from the cupboard.

"Danny is welcome to join us," she said, over her shoulder. "It's stir-fry."

"He won't be here."

"What's he up to?"

"I have no idea," I muttered. I set out the placemats and grabbed eight wooden chopsticks from the cutlery drawer. When I turned toward the table, Mom was giving me a worried look.

"Did something happen between you two?"

"No," I muttered, freaked out that her radar was that

good. "Can't we just have dinner with the four of us?"

She sighed. "Of course we can. It's just that I worry about that boy being by himself all the time."

I couldn't believe she was worried about *him*. "He's alone by *choice*, Mom. He's not like—" I began, but stopped myself.

She turned to look at me. "Not like what?" She paused. "Or who?"

"No one," I told her, counting out plates and napkins for the table. "It's nothing."

"*Steven*." She frowned. "I thought things were going well for you here."

Ha!

"Here in the house? Yup. I'm great in the kitchen and even better in the den."

She stared at me. "What does that mean? I thought you'd made some nice friends at school."

I took a deep breath. "Well, you thought wrong."

"*Steven*."

"I don't want to talk about it, okay?"

"But maybe I can help."

I thought back to the times she'd tried to help in the past. I didn't know a single kid at my own birthday party the year we were in Michigan. And Iowa? She set me up on a *play date* with the weirdest kid in school, who then convinced everybody that *I* was the weirdest.

I knew she had good intentions and she was only trying to help, but middle school was no place for moms.

"I'm finished with the table," I told her, moving away from it. "Can I go to my room?"

She sighed. "Fine."

I started toward the stairs, but realized I didn't want to go back to my room and hang out by myself. Instead, I walked into the living room, where Thomas was glued to the TV. He had his old headphones and microphone on and was busy talking to kids all over the country as they worked together, hunting zombies.

It wasn't enough that he'd already made real live friends. He had to be *virtually* popular too.

I could tell that the sound kept cutting out and that he was getting pretty frustrated. Despite my bad mood, I was glad I'd found him a new headset for Christmas.

"What, Steven?" Thomas suddenly asked.

"I didn't say anything."

"I know, but I can feel you."

"I'm not touching you," I snapped.

"No, not you, Choco-X," he said. "I'm talking to my brother." He paused, then said, "Steven."

"What?"

"Nothing. Someone just asked me your name." He paused again. "No, he doesn't play," he told the mystery person on the other end of the headset. Then he asked, "Do you want to play?"

I watched another zombie get splattered. Or maybe it was a vampire?

"Steven?"

"Yeah?"

"Do you want to or not?"

"What?"

"I asked if you wanted to play."

"Oh. I didn't know you were talking to me."

"Who else would I be talking to?"

"Some kid you've never met in Wyoming? Or maybe Texas?"

"What?"

"Never mind," I muttered and started toward the stairs.

"What's your problem?" Thomas asked.

I turned to see that he had one hand over his microphone, so no one could hear.

"Nothing," I said.

"You can totally play *Alien Blasters*, if you want."

Oh, they were *aliens*. "No thanks."

"You going snowboarding?"

"It's almost dinnertime."

"I mean tomorrow. If you need a buddy, I'll go."

"I'm just going to hang out here, I think."

His little purple avatar got blown up, but he didn't seem to notice.

"Seriously?"

"Seriously."

"Are you sick?" he asked.

"No. Look, I just don't feel like snowboarding, okay, Thomas?"

150

"Not okay," I heard him say quietly, as I climbed the stairs. "Totally weird."

It wasn't something I'd ever believe unless I'd lived it, but Christmas totally stunk. For starters, it turned out that Danny had called and told Mom he couldn't make it to dinner. He gave her some kind of an excuse, but I knew it was because he didn't want to hang out with me.

And on Christmas morning? Usually, Thomas and I would wake up when it was still dark out and race to grab our stockings, whispering and laughing the whole way. Then we'd jump on my parents' bed, waking them up (and probably scaring them a little). All four of us would open our stockings, taking turns unwrapping tiny packages while the others watched. Afterwards, Dad would make his awesome eggs Benedict and Thomas and I would try not to stare at all of the presents under the tree.

When we'd finished the meal and cleared everything away, we'd sit around the tree and Thomas would pass out the gifts. We'd all be happy and excited as we opened them, hugging and thanking each other, then we'd spend the rest of the day checking out our new stuff, watching movies and basically hanging out while the turkey cooked.

I loved it.

But that Christmas morning, everything was different.

I didn't wake up until Thomas knocked on my door.

"I'm sleeping," I groaned.

"Merry Christmas," he said, through the wood.

We hadn't spoken for the past two days and I was still annoyed with him, but it *was* Christmas.

"You too," I replied, but couldn't tell if he'd heard me.

I lay in bed for a minute, trying to feel the big swell of excitement that usually filled me up on Christmas morning, but it just felt like another day.

I rolled out of bed and by the time I got to Mom and Dad's room, everyone was waiting for me.

"Merry Christmas!" my parents shouted, pulling me into a group hug.

"Merry Christmas," I mumbled, my face jammed into Dad's armpit.

It was going to be a long day. I could feel it.

I liked all the stuff in my stocking, but it just wasn't as fun as usual to unwrap any of it. And instead of eggs Benedict, Dad decided to make French toast. It turned out he wasn't very good at it, and the whole time I was eating, I was daydreaming about the old days.

Of course, there were good parts too. Mom was even happier with her robe than I imagined and Dad was pretty stoked about the tool box we got him. Thomas was pumped about the new headset, and when it came time for me to open my big present from Mom and Dad, it turned out to be a bunch of clothes. Not, like, socks and underwear, but still pretty bad. Some pyjamas. A sweater. Some new jeans. Yes, there was a nice pair of snowboarding gloves that were on my list, *but still.*

I tried to hide my disappointment.

"Cool," I said, smiling. "Thanks, you guys."

I glanced at the tree and there was nothing left underneath it. I looked back at my pile of new clothes and couldn't help sighing.

"You haven't opened mine yet," Thomas said, handing me a small box.

I tore off the wrapping paper and pried open the plain brown cardboard. Inside was a tiny snowboard. A plastic one that I could hold in one hand.

Great.

"I made it," Thomas bragged. "Well, modified it, anyway. It's one of those fingerboards. I took off the wheels and painted it, just like the Green Beast."

Sure, if the Green Beast had been painted by someone with zero art skills. It was all smudged and didn't look anything like the original.

And what was I supposed to do with it?

"What's wrong?" Thomas asked.

"Nothing."

"You don't like it?"

"No, it's cool. Thanks, Thomas."

"Your brother put some real thought into that gift, Steven," Mom said, a bit of a warning in her voice.

"I know. I like it," I hurried to say.

Thomas frowned. "I know it's not like getting a real board, but—"

"It's better," I said, stunned that the words had come out of my mouth. "I can take it anywhere."

Dad handed his and Mom's coffee mugs to me. "Then you can take it with you when you grab us a refill."

I took the mugs and walked toward the kitchen, realizing this was the worst Christmas I'd ever had. The stuff at school, the mess with D-Day and the lamest presents ever. It was depressing.

But when I turned the corner, a huge wrapped box was leaning against the counter.

I stopped and stared at it.

We'd already opened everything.

Hadn't we?

My heart started to pound, because that box was a familiar size and shape. Long and rectangular.

I placed the mugs on the table and took a closer look, hoping for a name tag.

And there it was.

For Steven. Love from Santa.

"No way," I whispered.

"Way," Mom said, and when I spun around, my whole family was in the doorway, grinning.

"Seriously?" I asked, because it couldn't be.

"Open it!" they all said at once.

I started tearing at the paper.

"It's a cardboard box!" Thomas exclaimed. "You've always wanted one of those!"

"Very funny," I said, getting caught up in his excitement and laughing.

What if it was . . . ?

I kept yanking the paper away, and my heart started to beat a little faster when I saw a familiar logo.

Burton.

I swallowed hard, trying not to get my hopes up. Burton made a lot of stuff. Not just snowboards.

I tore away another strip.

The chances of me getting a new board after all of the expenses of moving were, like, nil.

Weren't they?

I ripped off the last bit of paper and stared at my gift for a few seconds before whispering, "You got me a new board?"

"Not just a new one," Thomas explained, "*the* new one."

I opened the box.

It was the Green Beast.

"Thank you," I murmured, through the lump in my throat. I got up to hug my parents and had to ask, "Are you sure?"

They both nodded and when she hugged me, Mom

said, "Dad told me how much you'd impressed him on the mountain."

"Thomas directed us to the right board," Dad said, and when I stopped hugging them, I hugged my little brother.

"We *so* had you going," he said, laughing.

"You totally did."

"You actually said the board I gave you was better than a real one!"

"I know," I said, letting go of him.

"That was hilarious, Steven."

Mom and Dad got busy in the kitchen, leaving Thomas and me in the living room.

"Thanks for telling Mom and Dad what I really wanted."

"No problem," my little brother said.

I looked at the stacks of cool stuff we'd all been given and wished Danny was coming for dinner so I could show him my awesome present.

It was funny to think that when Mom invited him, the first thing I'd thought about was what kind of a cool gift he might bring me.

And now? All I wanted was my friend back.

"You still mad at me?" Thomas asked, from his spot on the couch.

"Not really," I admitted. "What about you?"

"I wasn't mad," he said, shrugging.

He put on his headphones, turned on his console

and watched as the screen lit up. In just a few seconds, he was talking to some gamer in some other city, like it wasn't Christmas morning and I wasn't even there.

I leaned back against the cushions. Why was I surprised that our fight was one-sided? He didn't care enough about me to waste his time being mad. He was too busy with his thousands of friends.

And I couldn't even keep *one*.

"Why is it so easy for you?"

I was surprised to realize I'd asked the question out loud.

"What?" he asked, pulling off the headphones.

"Making friends. You do it like it's nothing. Like it's the easiest thing in the world."

He looked at me like I was crazy. "It is."

"Why?"

He laughed. "Because it doesn't matter."

"What are you talking about? It *totally* matters. Practically every year we move to a new place and start all over again. We have to meet new people and try to make friends and—"

"I don't."

I stared at him. "Don't what?"

"I don't have to try."

"That's my point. You meet these strangers and—"

"I already have a best friend."

"That's what I mean. Wait! A best friend? After less

than a *week*?" It was so unfair! How did a kid walk into a brand new school on Monday and have a best friend by Friday?

He rolled his eyes. "I'm talking about you, Steven."

I froze. "What?"

"You're my best friend."

"I am?"

He nodded. "It's cool to meet other kids and hang out and stuff, but I already have you."

I felt a lump in my throat. "We don't even go to the same school."

"So? Every time we move, I walk into a new classroom and see all those faces and I know you're doing the exact same thing. Whether we're in the same building or not, we're doing it together."

"But you have all of these friends . . ."

"And when we move again, we'll be in Montana or Iowa or whatever and they'll still be here. But you'll be with me. We'll have another first day of school and I'll walk into another classroom knowing that even if nobody likes me, I'll still see you at home and everything will be okay."

"But—"

"You're my *brother*, Steven. You're going to be my best friend for the rest of my life." He grinned. "Even if you stink at *Zombieville*."

I watched him play, shocked by what he had said. I had no idea he felt that way about me. That we were in it together. That I was his best friend.

After a few minutes he glanced at me. "I'm in an online tournament this week, so if you want to get some snowboarding in, you'd better call Danny."

I spent most of Monday moping around the house, bored and frustrated. Dad knocked on my bedroom door when he got home from work.

"Can I come in?" he asked, opening it a crack.

"Sure," I told him.

He sat on the end of my bed. "Mom says you haven't done anything all day."

"I emptied the dishwasher."

"I meant that you haven't left the house. She said you've barely been out of this room."

"There isn't anywhere I want to go."

Dad snorted. "Are you kidding me?"

"No."

His eyebrows gathered together. "But there's a world-class mountain with three inches of fresh powder a quarter of a mile from here."

I shrugged. "I just don't feel like it."

"Steven," he said, resting one hand on my shin. "You know you can always talk to me, about anything."

"I know."

"So, what's going on?"

I closed my eyes, so I wouldn't have to see the disappointment on his face when I said the dreaded words. "I don't have any friends."

He let go of my leg, and when I opened my eyes, I saw that he had pulled back in surprise. "Of course you do."

"No, Dad. I don't," I told him, embarrassed.

"No kids at school?"

"Nope."

"What about the ones we saw at the mall?"

"No."

"Well," he said, trying to get a grip on a problem I doubted he'd ever had. After all, he was a lot like Thomas. "What about Danny? He's your friend."

"Not anymore," I told him.

"Why not?"

I shrugged. "He got mad at me."

"*Mad at you?* What for?"

I sighed. "I wanted to introduce him to some people. It was no big deal."

"Introduce him to who?"

"Some kids from school."

Dad looked confused. "I thought you didn't have any friends at school."

"I don't. That's the whole point."

He shook his head. "I'm not following you, Steven."

I wasn't ready to tell him about the White Lie and how the whole mess got started, so I skipped that part and said, "I thought if they met a pro snowboarder . . ."

"I see," Dad said, nodding. "You wanted to show him off."

"No, I . . ." Wait. Did I? I guess maybe I *did* want to show him off. It just didn't sound so great when Dad put it that way.

"And Danny had already told you how much he wanted to be anonymous while he's up here," Dad added.

"Well, yeah."

"So?" he asked, eyebrows raised.

"So what?"

"Think about it, Steven."

So I did, for a solid couple of minutes. Finally, I realized something that made me feel rotten.

"He thinks I'm using him so I can be popular." I bit my lip and thought some more. "But I'm not. And it wasn't everybody, Dad. It was just a couple of kids from school." I groaned, totally frustrated. "I don't get why he has to be so private about everything."

"I thought you said he had a rough showing at the . . ."

"X Games," I finished for him. "Yeah, he did. He was trying to pull a Locust 1080, which is seriously awesome, but he blew it and . . . I mean, it was brutal. But that didn't mean he had to turn into a hermit."

Or did it?

How embarrassed would I have been, if it was me?

"Have you ever made a big mistake?" Dad asked.

I thought about the White Lie. "Yeah."

"In front of a bunch of people?"

I could still hear the crowd when I got called out as a liar. "Yeah."

"On television?"

"What? No." My humiliation would have been so much worse on TV!

"And I'll bet it's on YouTube."

For a split second, I thought he was talking about *my* mistake, and my stomach lurched. Then, I realized he was talking about Danny's Locust 1080.

"Yeah. It's had millions of views."

Dad gave me a long look. "So, if you made a big mistake in front of a live audience, as well as all of the people watching from home, and you knew that it would be watched by millions more people, whenever they felt like it on YouTube, you wouldn't want to hide out for a while?"

I had to admit, he made a good point. If I'd lived through that, I'd probably need more than a few days away from the spotlight.

But since I wasn't the one who'd blown the Locust 1080, I was able to look at the situation from a different perspective. And all I could think about was the fact that going underground wasn't really helping Danny at all.

If he wanted to get over the worst moment in his entire snowboarding career, he had to show everyone that his career wasn't over. That the missed 1080 was the fluke, not the tons of awesome runs and tricks that came before it.

As the thoughts raced in my mind, I grabbed my jacket and one other item and headed downstairs toward the front door.

"Where are you going?" Mom called.

"To see Danny!"

"Dinner's at six-thirty, Steven."

"Don't worry. I'll be back in time."

There was only one way (that I could think of) for Danny to get back on track.

He had to compete at the X Games again.

And it was up to me to convince him.

CHAPTER TWELVE

After a few minutes walking in the cold, I realized I should have brought gloves with me. And a hat. It was nice to be out, though. It had only been a couple of days, but it seemed like forever since I'd seen my breath blowing out in front of me and felt the burn of cold air in my lungs.

I glanced up at the mountain, wondering how packed the snow was up top. As soon as Christmas break was over and I was stuck in a classroom, I'd be kicking myself for wasting any of my time off inside the house.

After another ten minutes or so, I reached my destination.

The big gate.

If he'd wanted to hide, he definitely picked a good spot.

I walked up to the buzzer and pressed it, but I didn't hear anything. Did I have the right place? I pressed it a couple more times, but there was nothing. I kept tapping while I looked for another option.

"Enough with the buzzer!" a voice blasted through the speaker.

"Sorry!" I yelped, dropping my hand like I'd been burned. "I didn't think it worked."

"Then why did you keep hitting it?"

"Uh . . ." I didn't really have an answer for that. "Is this Danny?"

There was a long pause before the voice spoke again. "What do you want, Steven?"

"I, uh . . . I was wondering if I could talk to you for a minute."

"You are talking to me."

"I mean face to face. It's important."

There was another long stretch of silence before a beeping noise filled the air and the gate swung open.

I walked through it and started up a long, curved driveway until I reached a huge log cabin. Danny was standing in the open doorway.

We stared at each other.

"You coming in?" he finally asked.

It was probably the closest thing I'd get to an invitation, so I moved past him and into a bright kitchen.

He sat down at the counter and I picked the stool next to him.

I couldn't think of how to begin, so I just sat there, legs swinging in the silent room.

"So?" he finally asked.

"So what?"

"Uh, you're the one who wanted to talk to me. Remember?"

"Yeah," I cleared my throat. "Look, I'm sorry about what happened . . . with those guys from school. I know you're keeping a low profile right now because you missed that trick, but—"

He shook his head. "It's not just the trick, Steven."

I waited for him to say more, but he was quiet. I tried to imagine what else could be wrong. He had everything in the world going for him. The guy was getting paid to snowboard! Who the heck wouldn't want to be D-Day twenty-four hours a day?

"So . . . what's wrong?" I finally asked.

He sighed. "You wouldn't understand."

"Thanks a lot."

"Seriously, you're just a kid and—"

"So are you," I reminded him.

"Not really," he said, then took a deep breath before continuing. "I haven't felt like a kid for a long time."

More silence, until I asked, "What do you mean?"

"I don't know," he said, shaking his head. "This pro thing is a lot of pressure."

That made no sense. "Okay, my favourite hobby is your full-time job."

"Exactly."

"I mean, you get *paid* to snowboard, Danny. That's like, the most awesome thing ever."

He raised one eyebrow. "Not all the time."

"I don't get it," I admitted.

He got up and pulled a couple of cans of Power Blitz out of the fridge. He handed me one and cracked his open. "When I think back to how it was when I was a little kid, it feels like a hundred years ago. I *loved* snowboarding. It was all I wanted to do. No joke, if I wasn't on the mountain, I was daydreaming about the next time I'd be there."

"I know what you mean," I told him. "I never feel better than when I'm on that board."

He nodded. "So, I was winning local competitions, which was fun and cool and made me feel inspired to try more tricks. After a couple of years, I got a sponsor, then two more."

"Nice," I murmured, wishing I could tell the same story about myself someday.

"Yeah, it was cool, because it meant my mom didn't have to buy all of my gear anymore. Entry fees were paid for. We didn't have to worry so much about money."

"Free gear," I said, smiling. "That's pretty sweet."

"Definitely," he said. "And when I moved up to bigger competitions, there was prize money that came with winning a trophy."

"So cool!"

"Exactly. A dream come true, right?" He half-smiled. "Then I got bigger sponsors, competed more, and pretty soon I was making a lot of money." He glanced at me. "Like, a *lot* of money. More than I ever dreamed of."

I was having a hard time imagining how this story could possibly end badly.

"I was doing a lot of travelling and I had all kinds of photo shoots to do for magazine ads and commercials and stuff like that. Mom couldn't take care of all of my scheduling *and* work a full-time job, so she became my manager. And it was cool, because I could actually pay her more than she was making at her old job."

"Wow." I thought about how it would feel to pay my mom a salary. It would be weird, but it would probably feel pretty good too.

"It was perfect. She took care of all the details, travelled with me, home-schooled me and helped me make some pretty major decisions."

I waited, but he'd stopped talking again.

"So, what happened?"

"Matrix happened."

What was that supposed to mean? They made goggles and gloves and stuff. "Another sponsor," I said.

"Yeah. Another sponsor." He sounded depressed.

"But that's good, right?"

"Sure, if you happen to like Matrix gear."

I shrugged. "It's what you always wear."

"It's what I *have to* wear."

"Huh?"

"When companies decide to sponsor you, they give you money and pay for stuff, but they expect certain things in return. My Matrix contract says I can't wear any other goggles or gloves."

"Or?"

"Or I get fined thousands and thousands of dollars."

"Whoa."

He sighed. "I'd worn the same style of Oakleys since day one on a snowboard. I had a bunch of pairs and I just swapped them out when they got old or scratched up."

"Like my old ones. The ones you borrow all the time."

"Yeah. You know, they felt so good and familiar on me that first day we hung out, it was like I was just a kid snowboarding again."

"But if someone sees you wearing them?"

He frowned. "I'll be fined. That's the thing, Steven. Mom thought this Matrix deal was too good to pass up. We signed the contract right before the X Games." He glanced at me and looked kind of embarrassed. "It's kind of dumb, but those old Oakleys were my *lucky* goggles."

"And you couldn't wear them," I finished for him. I'd never thought sponsorship could be a *bad* thing.

"Exactly. It totally psyched me out. So, there I am, wearing goggles I don't like, promoting drinks I can't stand." He raised his Power Blitz like he was toasting me. "Using gear that didn't feel right . . . and then I bomb at the X Games."

I wanted to tell him he hadn't bombed, but we both knew the truth.

"You know," he continued, "sometimes I think things would be a lot different if I wasn't a pro."

"They would," I told him, thinking of the mess I'd made of middle school. "Trust me."

"Hey, are you hungry?" he asked. "I've got some frozen hot dogs we could microwave."

I shook my head, glad that stir-fry was on the menu at home. "No, thanks."

He pulled out a frozen brick of dogs and worked at getting two loose with a knife. Once the microwave was whirring, he said, "There was this girl who lived a couple of houses down from me in Denver."

"A snowboarder?" I asked.

"No—"

"Skier?"

"No."

"Was she a—"

"She was just a girl, okay?" He shook his head. "Anyway, her name was Cari. I really liked her and I was pretty sure she liked me." He sighed. "But then I started doing all of this travelling and things changed."

"Yeah, you had a bunch of money and you were famous."

"Exactly," he said, quietly. "We were keeping in touch by text and phone, which was really cool. In fact, everything was going great until she saw me on TV, surrounded by a bunch of screaming girls."

It sounded like a horror movie. "Ugh."

"They were cute girls, Steven."

"Still ugh."

He rolled his eyes. "Anyway, I tried to explain to Cari that I didn't even know those girls and they were just doing it for the camera. Then Missy Dillons—"

"The singer?"

"Yeah. She told some interviewer that we were dating, and once Cari heard that, she didn't want to have anything to do with me."

"But you *weren't* dating Missy Dillons?"

How the heck had I gotten into a conversation about *dating*?

"Nope."

The microwave beeped and Danny pulled out his plate and squeezed a big blob of ketchup onto it. He dipped a dog and took a bite, then continued, "All of the TV and magazine stuff, and all of the girl 'fans' were too much for Cari and that was it."

"That's too bad," I told him, trying to look sad.

But to be honest, this wasn't exactly a *sad* story. I didn't hate girls or anything. They usually smelled pretty good and they were nicer than guys about some stuff. But I'd way, way, way rather be a pro snowboarder than have a girlfriend. I mean, *come on*.

"So, the point is, I wonder what would have happened if I'd just stayed a regular kid in a regular school."

He had to be kidding.

"Nothing!" I exclaimed. "Nothing would have happened. You'd have gone to Math class and English class and spent your lunch hour in the cafeteria. Just like me, you would have sat there, wishing like crazy that you were a pro boarder instead of a nobody."

"You aren't a nobody, Steven." He took another bite of his hot dog.

"Sure I am."

"No," he said, smiling. "*Everyone* knows who you are."

"Very funny." I sighed. "They only know who I am because I did something stupid."

"So, instead of famous, you're infamous."

I was quiet for a minute, trying to figure out what I wanted to say.

"I'm sorry I've been such a jerk, Danny." Before he could respond, I told him, "It was totally stupid and immature to tell that lie, then I tried to pull you into it. That was pretty lame and I feel bad about it. I should have just . . . been myself instead."

He nodded. "I'll bet there are hundreds of kids at that school, right?"

I shrugged. "I guess."

"So at least one or two of those kids could probably use a friend. Even if he *isn't* Cody White's cousin."

"Maybe," I said, hoping he was right.

"I want you to promise me something, Steven."

"What?"

"Promise me that when school starts, you'll sit next to somebody in the cafeteria."

"Uh . . ." I pictured the sea of kids, all sitting in their own special seats, talking, eating and joking around. Would somebody let me squeeze onto the end of their bench?

Maybe.

"Okay."

"And talk to them."

"What?" I practically choked.

"Talk to them," he repeated, then seemed to re-think it. "No. Scratch that. You can't do all the talking. You need to have an actual conversation with them."

"With who?" I gasped. "About what?"

"Whoever is there." He smiled. "You can talk snowboarding, but you also have to find out something about them and what they're into."

"How am I supposed to . . . Are you kidding me?"

He shook his head. "Nope."

"But Danny—"

"It's not that big a deal, Steven. People do it every day."

"Yeah. Other people."

"And I want you to do something else too."

"Seriously?"

"You also have to join a school club."

"What?" I croaked.

"You heard me. When I was in school, I was in the Outdoors Club, and I worked on the student website."

I slumped in my chair. "Oh, man."

"Promise me."

I thought about it for a minute. "Fine. But you have to promise me something too."

"What?" he asked, suspiciously.

"That you'll compete at the X Games." I paused. "Next month."

"It's too late," he said, shrugging.

"No, it isn't."

"Steven, come on. Do you have any idea how long training takes?"

"Yeah, but it's not like you're starting from *scratch*. You're already an awesome snowboarder. You blew one trick, one time and—"

"And it happened to be on TV."

"And it'll be on YouTube for the next hundred years. So what?"

He raised one eyebrow. "Well, I know millions of viewers aren't *nearly* as bad as a couple of hundred kids seeing you make a fool of yourself in a middle-school cafeteria . . ."

"Okay. But you don't actually *see* those millions of viewers every day." I paused. "Look, I have a chance to change things after Christmas break, just like you at the X Games. You have a chance to show everybody what you can do."

"Steven—"

"Look, I may not make all of the best decisions and I admit I've made some dumb mistakes, but I know snowboarding. You could make a total comeback."

He gave me a doubtful look. "And make you a hero?"

"No! No, it's got nothing to do with me. I know you love boarding as much as I do and I don't want to see you miss out. I don't care if no one ever knows that I met you and that we hung out. I just want you to get that medal, Danny. You deserve it."

"Thanks, but it's not going to happen. It's too soon. I won't be ready to—"

"I could train you—"

He choked on a mouthful of hot dog. "Hold on. What did you just say?"

"I could train you."

"*Steven.*"

"What? I've probably watched that missed trick more than you have. I know what you did wrong and—"

"I didn't have enough speed going into the rotations."

"Uh . . . yeah," I said, surprised he'd said exactly what I'd been about to.

He rolled his eyes. "That wasn't my first day on a board, you know."

"I know," I admitted. "Okay, so I couldn't *train* you, but I could help you. I mean, competing again could change everything."

"I don't know," he said, hesitating.

"You've had fun on the mountain with me, right?"

"Yeah," he said, giving me a suspicious look.

"Because we were just two guys, hanging out."

He nodded. "Exactly."

"Old Oakley goggles and no fans at the bottom of the run."

"Yeah. It was really cool."

"So, let's just keep doing what we've been doing."

He stared at me. "How's that supposed to prepare me for the X Games?"

"By bringing the *fun* back into it. No managers, no sponsors, no TV cameras. Just you, me, our boards and fresh powder."

"I don't know," he said, but I could tell he was starting to think about the possibilities. "The X Games are coming up pretty fast." He looked out the window, squinting at the peak of the mountain and obviously thinking it over. "I guess if I skipped Boardercross and Slopestyle—"

"You could concentrate on Big Air," I finished for him.

"Well, it *is* my best event."

I nodded. "There you go," I told him. "Start strong."

He took another sip of Power Blitz, made a horrible face and emptied the can in the sink.

"Maybe I could update a comfortable old combo. Add a couple of tricks, you know?"

"Why not?" I said, getting excited. "No one says you have to try the Locust 1080 again."

He let out a long, slow breath. "But it would be pretty cool if I did." He smiled at me. "And nailed it."

"Yeah," I had to agree. "It would be epic."

We were quiet for a minute and the only sound was a ticking clock somewhere in the house.

"What's gotten into you?" Danny finally asked.

"What do you mean?"

"I don't know. A few days ago all you cared about was whether the kids at school thought you were cool."

I thought about the conversations I'd had with Thomas and Dad and all of the thinking I'd done on my own.

"I guess I've been looking at things differently."

"That's good," he said. "I like it." He shook his head. "You know what? I'm going to do it."

"Seriously?"

"Yes. I can't believe you talked me into this," he said, laughing.

I couldn't believe it either. I checked the clock and was about to head home for dinner when I felt something in my pocket.

"Oh! I forgot the other thing I want you to promise me for the X Games."

"It's a two-parter, huh?"

"Yeah," I said, pulling my old Oakleys from my coat pocket. "You have to promise me you'll wear these."

CHAPTER THIRTEEN

As soon as Danny's mom and coach found out that he wanted to compete at the X Games, they decided to fly him to Utah for some intense training and practice.

That was totally *not* what I wanted to happen, but I knew it was for the best. I hid my disappointment that he was leaving and focused on how cool it was that he was getting back into the sport.

"Well, good luck to you," Dad said, when Danny stopped by the house to say goodbye.

"Thanks," Danny said, as Mom pulled him into a hug.

"Don't blow it this time," my little brother advised.

"Thomas!" Mom, Dad and I all gasped.

Danny nodded to him. "Thanks for the tip."

The rest of my family left us alone and we stood in the hallway in silence.

"So, this is it, huh?" I asked.

"Only for now," he said, smiling. "This is one of my favourite places."

"Good runs," I said, nodding.

"Good people too."

I cleared my throat, preparing to ask the question I'd been dying to know the answer to.

"Have you thought about the Locust 1080?"

"Have you thought about your first day back at school?" he countered.

"Yeah." Even though I tried not to. Every time I imagined all of the faces staring at me in the cafeteria, my hands started to sweat. "You're seriously not going to tell me if you're doing it?"

He shook his head. "You'll have to wait and see, like everybody else."

School started just a few days later and I woke up feeling nervous and jittery.

"Want to walk with me?" Thomas asked, when I met him in the kitchen after I'd showered and dressed.

"Sure," I told him, dropping a couple of slices of whole wheat in the toaster. By the time it popped, I had the peanut butter open and ready to spread.

"Are you freaked out?"

"About school?" I asked, and when he nodded I admitted, "Kind of."

"It'll be fine."

"What will be fine?" Mom asked, stopping in to refill her mug of coffee.

"School," I told her.

"Of course it will."

I hoped she was right and kept on hoping while I ate my breakfast, packed my bag and said goodbye to Thomas at his school turnoff.

I took a deep breath and set my sights on the low brick building in front of me. As I walked toward it, my Vans crunched in the snow and I knew I'd be wearing cold, wet socks for the rest of the day.

A bike whipped past me, almost grazing my shoulder. Nolan, of course.

He stopped and turned toward me. "Cody White's cousin," he sneered.

"Nope."

He shook his head. "What a loser."

I pretended it didn't bother me and kept on walking. When I was within a few feet of him, he snorted and rode off. It was going to be a long day.

I tried to blend in with the stream of kids heading for the front doors. There were a few whispers and laughs, but I'd been expecting that.

At my locker, I unloaded what I could from my pack, my back to all of the chatter in the hallway. I tried to convince myself that one day I'd be part of it all, but it was tough.

In homeroom, I sat at the back and only looked up when my name was called for attendance. A few kids swivelled in their seats to look at me or snicker, but I only felt my face heat up a little bit.

I made it through my morning classes, barely saying a word, but when the lunch bell rang, I knew that was about to change.

As much as I wanted to hide out and eat in peace, I knew I had to honour my promise to Danny. I had to sit down next to somebody and have a real conversation.

I could feel the sweat on the back of my neck as I gathered my lunch and started toward the cafeteria.

The volume got louder the closer I got, and by the time I reached the open doors, I was overwhelmed by the buzz of conversation.

I took a deep breath, clutching my lunch bag tightly, and scanned the room.

Practically every seat was taken already, and my heart started to pound. I hovered in the doorway, looking for an empty space.

"Are you going in or what?" someone grunted from behind me, and I stumbled into the room.

It felt like every pair of eyes in the place was on me. People nudged each other and tilted their heads at me. They pointed their fingers, whispered behind their hands and flat-out stared.

I promised Danny.

I promised myself.

I thought about Thomas, eating his lunch at the elementary school, and breathed a little easier. We were doing it together.

I reached the end of the first row and moved to the second, which seemed just as crowded.

After about ten steps, I saw an opening and moved toward it. The kids had their backs to me, so I cleared my throat.

"Uh, is it okay if I sit here?"

When the girl spun around, I recognized her.

It was Glitter Morgan.

And she was smiling.

"Sure," she said. "Hey guys, scoot down a bit for Steven."

To my total amazement, they did.

"Thanks," I said, settling in next to her.

"No problem. Did you have a good Christmas?"

"Yeah," I told her, pulling my sandwich out of the bag. "It was really good." I remembered what Danny had said about making conversation. "How was yours?"

"Perfect," she said. "My cousins were visiting and things got pretty crazy."

"Where are they from?" I asked, taking a bite of my sandwich.

"Colorado."

"I used to live there," I told her.

"You used to live everywhere," she said, laughing.

"Hey, have you met Jace?" she asked, pointing to the guy sitting next to her.

"No."

"He's a snowboarder too." She elbowed him and introduced us.

"Cody White's cousin," he said, chuckling.

I felt my ears get hot. "Not really," I admitted.

He smiled, but not in a mean way. "I know."

We each took a bite of our food and chewed in silence.

"I think I saw you on the mountain during break," Jace said. "I was on the lift and you were with a guy in all black."

The old me would have told him that the guy was none other than legendary pro snowboarder D-Day.

The new me just said, "Yeah, that's a friend of mine."

"He was really good." Jace took another bite of his apple. "You were too."

"Thanks," I told him, smiling. "Maybe we could go together sometime," I said, hoping I didn't sound weird or desperate.

"Yeah. That would be cool."

It seemed like lunch had just started when the bell rang and as I got up from the table I couldn't stop smiling.

A few weeks later, my whole family was gathered around the TV to watch the X Games, something that never would have happened if I hadn't met Danny.

We'd spoken on the phone a couple of times, which was awesome. He'd talked about how well his training was going and how he wanted to make some changes in his career. He'd spoken to his mom about all of the sponsorships and endorsements, and the two of them were going to meet with a lawyer to see what kind of options they had. He was even thinking about calling that girl he liked, but he hadn't done it yet.

"Did I miss anything?" Thomas asked, hurrying into the room after a bathroom break.

"It's just about to start."

I'd watched the Big Air semifinals earlier in the day, and I'd seen Danny edge out Cotter Lowry for third place. He hadn't tried the Locust 1080, but he'd managed a pretty sweet Double Backside Rodeo, and the crowd had gone crazy.

He didn't look *happy* with third, but it was all he needed to make the top five for the final.

Which was starting now.

Mom had made a big bowl of popcorn, but I had zero appetite. I was too worried about what was going to happen. Of course, I knew Danny was an awesome boarder and could do pretty much any trick he put his mind to. But would he be willing to put his mind to a Locust 1080?

Man, I hoped so.

Dad passed the popcorn to Thomas, who chewed

louder than anything I'd ever heard. I grabbed the remote and cranked the volume, not wanting to miss a second of the action.

First up was Jack Alvarez. I wasn't worried about him at all because he'd never placed higher than fifth at an event like this.

"I like the jacket," Mom said.

"And the boots," Thomas added, through a mouthful of popcorn.

"Okay, this isn't a fashion show, you guys."

The doorbell rang and I jumped up to answer, knowing it was for me. When I swung the door open, Ethan and Morgan were on the front step.

"Are we late?" Morgan asked.

"You're just in time," I told her, as I led them into the living room.

"Hey, kids!" Mom called from the couch. "Help yourselves to snacks and drinks."

My new friends got settled in front of the TV.

"This will be over in time for choir practice, right?" Ethan asked.

"Yeah," I told him. "My dad will give us a ride."

Yes, I had joined the Evergreen School Choir.

And yes, it was surprisingly awesome.

"Here we go!" Thomas shouted.

I held my breath as Danny got into position at the top of the ramp. I saw that he was wearing my goggles. Just like me, he'd kept his promises.

I was super-nervous as I watched him do a couple of squats to warm up his legs.

The camera went in for a close-up, and I could tell he was worried. He was frowning slightly and staring off into the distance, like there was a storm coming.

I just hoped the storm was *him*.

He spread his arms out in a wide stretch and then shook them out.

You can do this.

"He looks nervous," Thomas said.

"I'm sure he is." The next couple of minutes would either be the biggest comeback the sport had ever seen . . . or something else. Something I didn't even want to think about. Like a disaster.

Come on, Danny. You've got this.

"What happens if he messes up?" Thomas asked.

"He's not going to mess up," I told him, my voice firm. "And even if his first jump isn't perfect, they average the scores on two jumps."

"He gets two tries?" Ethan asked.

"Two tries," I repeated.

It would all come down to two big jumps. Just a few seconds in the air.

He was an awesome snowboarder. A pro, who'd been on a board for almost his whole life. He was no stranger to tough competition and he really wanted to win.

He wasn't going to mess up.

I barely heard the announcer listing off his stats,

and when he started talking about the last X Games, I stopped listening.

I watched Danny roll his shoulders and bend his knees a couple more times.

He looked ready to go for it.

And then he dropped in!

He looked smooth and solid on his way down the ramp, totally focused on the jump ahead of him. He shifted to his left, getting himself in position.

Six seconds later, he rode up, up, up the jump and shot off the top.

It was awesome!

A backside triple cork, his board and body soaring and swirling through the air so fast it was hard to count the rotations.

"A 1620!" the announcer exclaimed as Danny made a rough landing but stayed upright.

"He started with the easy one," I whispered.

"A 1080 is harder?" Thomas asked, doubtfully.

"Yeah. This one has more rotations, but the Locust is a harder trick. You know, if he does it."

My eyes were glued to the screen as Danny waited for his score.

"Only forty-two?" Glitter Morgan gasped.

"It's out of fifty," I explained.

"Whew," she said.

Danny raised his hand at the cheering fans, but didn't pump his arm in victory.

Because it wasn't over yet.

We waited impatiently as the rest of the competitors did their thing. I couldn't eat a thing, but everyone else chomped on popcorn like we were watching an action movie.

By the time Danny was up again, my stomach was in knots.

He went through his usual warm-up moves, his gaze still steady. This time, instead of frowning, there was a hint of a smile on his face, like he knew something awesome was about to happen.

I held my breath as he dropped in and sailed downward, looking like the board was part of his body.

He shot up the jump, faster than the first time, like he needed more speed and bigger air.

Like he was preparing for a Locust 1080.

Yes!

He hauled off the jump, tucking and spinning so quickly it was like we were watching in fast-forward. My heart was racing and I felt like *I* was the one pulling the trick.

My hands were clenched as he passed the point where he'd crashed the last time, my nails digging into my palms when the board touched down and he slid to an absolutely perfect stop.

The TV was silent. The room was silent.

Everyone knew we'd just witnessed something incredible.

"He did it!" I shouted, waving my arms and sending the popcorn bowl flying. "He really did it!"

His score was a forty-nine.

He was winning the gold, for sure.

The gold!

I watched in awe as the camera hurried over to him, the reporter panting with either excitement, breathlessness, or both.

"So, how do you feel?" she asked.

Danny looked the happiest I'd ever seen him. His grin covered his whole face and his eyes were shining.

His voice shook a little as he said, "I'm totally amped right now. It was an *awesome* run. I mean, everything about it felt good." He took a breath. "I want to thank my coach, Kate Winnows, my parents and all the fans out there who kept rooting for me."

"That's you," Dad whispered, nudging me with his foot.

I waited for Danny to start listing sponsors, but he didn't do it. It was a pretty bold move and I hoped he wouldn't get in too much trouble.

"Any last words?" the reporter asked.

"Yeah," Danny said, with a nod. "I want to thank a good friend of mine, back in Oregon."

No way.

No way!

"Steven White."

Morgan gasped, and I put my hand on her arm so I could hear the rest.

"He's the one who made me go for the 1080." Then he looked right into the camera and said, "Thanks, Steven."

"Yes! I bet a bunch of kids from school saw *that*," Thomas said, gleefully.

"It doesn't matter," I said, grinning.

And that was the truth.

I didn't care who knew that I was friends with Danny, or that he'd given me a shout-out on national TV.

I was just happy for *him*.

And when I looked around the room, from my parents to my best friend, Thomas, to two of the *five* new friends I'd already made at school, I realized something pretty cool.

I was happy for me too.

ABOUT THE AUTHOR

W.C. Mack was born in Vancouver, B.C., and now lives in Portland, Oregon. She has always been a Canucks fan, and eventually combined her love of sports with her love of writing. She has written stories featuring hockey, basketball and soccer, and her book *Athlete vs. Mathlete* has been nominated for children's choice awards in Canada and around the world.

In her spare time she can be found cheering on her favourite teams at arenas, gridirons and diamonds across North America.

MORE GREAT SPORTS BOOKS BY W.C. MACK

Hat Trick
ISBN 978-1-4431-0201-8

Breakaway
ISBN 978-1-4431-1942-9

Line Change
ISBN 978-1-4431-0784-6

MORE GREAT SPORTS
BOOKS BY W.C. MACK

Athlete vs. Mathlete
ISBN 978-1-4431-1361-8

Tag Team
ISBN 978-1-4431-2828-5